Mistress Treat

"Debby? Are you ready? It's past eight."

Her muffled words he took for invitation and he was in the little bedroom before she could protest.

She stood in frilly pantalets that clung tightly to the turn of her hips and fell in little ruffles of lace about her thighs. Tight silk stockings encased her legs and black ribbon garters indented her flesh.

She cried out and turned, offering him a nude white back.

"Debby," he whispered.

She looked at him over a bared shoulder, seemingly unaware that she stood before a mirror.

"I did say I'd be your doxy, Colonel, but I never thought you'd treat me like one."

He fought the hunger in him, but the hunger won and he crossed the room to her.

"You teased me all the way from Charlotte!" he whispered.

"The way you wanted me to tease you."

His hands turned her and brought her against him, her mouth so close he only had to bend to kiss her. Then she wrenched away, burying her face in his chest. "Leave me to my dressing, or we'll never reach the officers' ball!"

"Dress yourself, then!" he cried hoarsely. "Make yourself as lovely as you can to tempt those damned turncoats and lobsterbacks!"

REBEL WENCH

Gardner F. Fox

WILDSIDE PRESS

www.wildsidepress.com

REBEL WENCH

Chapter One

THE KEY turned in the lock and the door opened on the room he had not seen for more than four years. The low ceiling, slanting slightly where it reached out toward the gable window, the faded pattern of the Chinese wallpaper, the big spool bed with its crazy-quilt covering, all were as he remembered them. Gray dust lay thick over everything, as if to hide his secret from the world.

The man moved into the room and closed the white pine door softly behind him. A smile tugged at the corners of his wide mouth. Ben Leap had oiled the hinges, as he had been told to do. The man paused a moment, his eyes sliding to the heavy iron-banded chest that stood below a long Elliott mirror on the wall. Then he was striding to the dormer window, lifting the shade, letting sunlight come into the room. He set the long Kentucky rifle he carried gently on the floor.

The sunlight gilded the white buckskin hunting shirt he wore, with its fringes at sleeves and back, and slid across the green sash about his middle that marked him for one of Morgan's Rifles. Under the sash was a wide leather belt that held his shot pouch and long knife. He was a tall man, and lean. The breadth of his shoulders stretched the buckskin tight to the muscles that rippled as he lifted the hunting shirt and threw it from him.

5

He knelt and worked at the lock on the big chest. Dust rose in a little cloud as he threw back the ironbound top and revealed the blue velvet jacket and breeches and lawn shirt, the riding boots and frilled jabot. A smile twisted the corners of his mouth as he drew out the frock coat and held it up.

Billy Joe Stafford felt a twist of regret for the might-have-been. Four years in the North, fighting in Morgan's company against the English lobsterbacks, from Quebec right down through Monmouth and the seemingly endless little fights that followed that debacle. That long, endless winter in Valley Forge. His arm twitched where a white scar marked it: the scar a British saber had put in his flesh on Christmas night of '77. Four years! Four years without Laura Lee in his arms, without her wide, moist mouth to soothe away his hurts and hungers, without her pale body to entice his senses in the great bedchamber at Stafford Hall.

The thought of Laura Lee Stafford, that sultry beauty who was his wife, put a tempest of impatience in his blood. He stood and worked at the green sash, at the wide leather belt and deerskin leggins. Naked, he bent to the chest and drew out linen shirt and cravat, breeches and boots.

He dressed, remembering the day in '73 he had brought Laura Lee Moulton to Stafford Hall, which his grandfather had built in 1723. Lord, but she had been a temptation in her nightrail, laughing and running from him, bringing him French wines in a crystal beaker and goblet, standing like that in a shaft of revealing moonlight, maddening him. For three years, he and Laura Lee had been lovers. Then word had gone south from Lexington and Concord: The colonies were in rebellion! He himself had been eager to get away, to ride to Fredericksburg and join the company Dan Morgan was gathering: Virginia rifles, and each man of them a sharpshooter. His wife refused to let him go. Laura Lee was a royalist, a Tory.

Her white face swam before his remembering eyes. Her full mouth was pinched to a thin red line and her dark eyes blazed hotly at him. Her voice was rasping. "You're insane. Insane! You know that, don't you?"

Her ringed hand gestured, making him see the pillared majesty of the Hall, its white outbuildings with their blue roofs and trim, the fields of wheat and cotton, the sleek, fast horses in the west meadows and the herds of cows that would be ambling now through the early dusk, back to their big, clean barns.

"You'd give up all this to ride with a pack of ragamuffins to fight against your king! With a ragtail mob! And what for? To find yourself face down someday on a field or in a ditch, with your blood oozing out! Dying! You don't expect to gain anything from this little rebellion?"

His smile had been a patient thing. In the years of his marriage to Laura Lee, he had learned patience. "The King taxes us blind. His ministers come stalking with their noses in the air, arrogant as peacocks. They take our pride as they take our money. Our English agents conspire with each other to short-change our every shipment. They treat us worse than we treat the slaves!"

She flung mocking laughter at him. "Tell the rest of the world all that, Billy Joe. Tell me the truth! Tell me that the Stafford blood runs hot in your veins! The same blood that drove your grandfather into seven duels, until the eighth one killed him. The same blood that haunted your father through the last two wars with France, in '48 and '56! That gave him the chest trouble that killed him."

He said softly, "Because of all that, you find yourself mistress of the richest plantation in the Dan River country."

"And I want to keep what I have, Billy Joe! Not just the plantation, but you as well!"

She had thrown herself into his arms then, and the weight of her soft, fragrant flesh and the touch of her hungry mouth had silenced him. He had been a coward. He had crept from her bed in the early hours of the morning while she lay sleeping placidly, had donned this blue velvet riding suit and written her a letter, then ridden off on one of the plantation's big stallions to his room at Ben Leap's ordinary.

Now he was coming back, unheralded and unannounced, four years later.

Billy Joe Stafford stared at his reflection in the mirror on the wall. He had put weight on his chest and arms and legs in those four years. His shirt and jacket and breeches were tight to bursting with his added bulk. The pale yellow of his hair seemed almost white against the dark mahogany of his tanned face. The Stafford nose, high and thin, and the Fairfax blue eyes and dimpled chin, which were an inheritance from his mother, mocked at his beating heart.

Will she be waiting? The words that came up from his very depths, in answer to each throbbing heartbeat, taunted him. He knew the pride that ran in Laura Lee. He had hurt that pride by running away. Now, in this November, 1780, he was coming home, to learn if her pride was still as fierce.

With steady hands he set the gold-laced tricorn more firmly on his head, then paused for one last glance about the little room that had been his since his sixteenth birthday. His father had paid a year's rent on it, giving it to him for a birthday present, telling him a man needed to get off by himself once in a while, away from his troubles. He had sat on the edge of that big canopied bed, staring as he saw his first woman undress for him, remembering the bayberry candle hanging on a rung of the ladder-back chair where his foot was propped, casting shadows across her slender thighs. Beyond it, in a nook under the slanted ceiling, was the writing desk where he had sat for three hours the day his father died. It had been on that desk that he had first composed the letter he had slipped under Laura's pillow, the night he ran away. Aye, he told himself bitterly, the room was filled with memories for him, but it was not those memories that held him here. It was the fear in his middle, the fear that made him linger.

He was afraid to face Laura Lee.

"What will she be like?" he whispered. "Will she welcome me back or turn me over to the Tories? Is the plantation a ruin? Did she go back to Charles Town, where I married her?"

A hand on the knob of the door, a wrench, and he was out in the hall, breathing harshly, feeling the lawn shirt cut into his shoulders from its tightness. "She's my wife!" he told the heavy canvas floor cloth on the hall plankings.

Then the stair was underfoot and he was leaping downward, anxious now to see her, and to learn what was waiting for him at Stafford Hall.

He came into the taproom from the inner hall, not seeing the huge brick fireplace with its brass andirons and fireback gleaming from their years of polishing, the long fowling piece and carved powder horn on leather thongs and wooden pegs above it. A few fiddle-backed rockers stood between the hearth and a large trestle table in the middle of the room. In the west corner, taking up more than half the wall, was the planked bar, its slatted corner railing reaching upward to the beamed ceiling.

Stafford moved through the room and out onto the stone slabs that served as steps to the entry door. Early-afternoon sunlight showed him the road stretching off toward the Dan and Stafford Hall. Bermuda grass and low evergreens made a sea of green beyond the road, as far away as the Blue Ridge Mountains. The sound of trotting hoofs and the whinny of a horse made him turn and come down onto the graveled carriage drive.

Ben Leap, who ran the Black Thistle ordinary, came around the corner of the house, the reins of a big bay stallion in his large hand. A grin distorted his plump cheeks. His white head bobbed, but not before Stafford saw a fresh bruise on his lined cheek.

"A new horse every month," he told Stafford. "Brought by Old Gem, who comes every week to curry him, and exercise him on the road yonder."

Stafford smiled to cover the lump in his throat. Old Gem had been slave to his father and his grandfather before him, and had taught him to sit a saddle and handle a frisky mount. It would be like Old Gem to keep coming back, week after week and month after month for four years, certain that his master would return someday.

He was reaching for the black leather rein when a man shouted with laughter inside the tavern. There was something lewd in the manner of that laugh. It was followed by a sob and the sharp cry of an angry woman.

Ben Leap flushed. The bruise on his cheek stood out darker against the tide of blood. When he caught Stafford's inquisitive glance, the old man grimaced. "A damned Yankee. Roaring drunk last night, sir. Put this mark on my phiz with a beer cup when I asked for manners."

The woman screamed, and Stafford relaxed his grip on the rein. He said softly, staring at the door of the ordinary's long room, "There's teacher's blood in me at the moment, Ben. I've a mind to show this Yankee how we behave to a woman this far south."

The old man said, "He's a mean one, sir. Big and heavy. With a slant to his eye that I mislike."

Stafford nodded. "I've seen his kind before. First to join when the battle is won, first to go when the fighting gets rough." His hands rose to his blue velvet frock coat. He removed it and put it across the saddle. As he walked toward the long-room door, his fingers worked busily, rolling up the sleeves of his lawn shirt.

He came into the long room, with its twin fireplaces and small trestle tables, ladder-back chairs and hanging Betty lamps. A blonde girl in a homespun dress of green wool that was ripped from a white shoulder and torn half-way up her leg was sprawled across the knee of a big man, whose fleshy face was thrust deep in her throat. His big hands were fondling the girl even as her fingers clawed at his shoulder. Her right hand left his arm and tangled its fingers in his thick black hair, tugging savagely. Her breathing was hoarse and frantic.

Whether it was her hand in his hair lifting his head or the sound of Stafford's top boots on the floor that stayed the man, Stafford never knew. The big man raised his head and stared at him, and his loose mouth sneered. He was fleshy, with tangled black hair and pig eyes, and his teeth showed rotten when he sneered.

"A gentleman farmer come to save your virtue, girl! As if you've any left to salvage!"

He pushed the girl from him, thrust her rolling across the floor with a foot. With a curse for Stafford, he brought his big pewter beaker to his lips and swallowed noisily. Before he was finished drinking, he took the beaker from his mouth and hurled it in a movement curiously fluid for such a big man.

Stafford heard the girl scream as the beaker caught him at his cheek and gashed a bloody furrow. Then the big man was coming for him, rolling the table from his path with a big hand at its edge, his feet pounding dust from the floor boards as he came.

Stafford slid aside from the bullish rush, and his fists went out, left and right, slamming into the big man at jaw and belly, turning him around to face him. A fist brought blood from the wide nose and opened the corner of his lips. The fleshy man blinked a little stupidly. Slowly, the stupidity of surprise gave way to a rush of anger that mottled his cheeks. He roared and lowered his head and charged.

The Staffords were big of bone, with thick sinew on them, but this Northern giant outweighed Billy Joe by twenty pounds. He was fat, but the ease with which he had swung the table from him showed he was strong under his blubber. Stafford rode before his rush, fighting as he had fought in camp fights from Canada all the way to New Jersey. He used his fists as a duelist uses his point. He jabbed until blood trickled from an eye and gushed from a nose. He flailed at the man's belly until he fought for breath, wetly, bent far over.

The big man was a knowing fighter. He gave out punishment too, so that Stafford felt on fire where a huge fist raked the side of his face, and where an iron poker tore a gash in his side as the man swung it wildly.

Vaguely Stafford was aware of the blonde girl, crouched on the floor and staring at them with wide eyes. Once he saw her rise to her knees, when two right-hand blows doubled up the big man. Her fingers fell from the torn green gown they held together over her bosom to ball into a fist, and he caught a flashing glimpse of a thin golden chain and the locket it suspended.

"Kill the pig!" he heard her whisper. "Kill him for what he did to me!"

Stafford did not kill him, but he beat him to his knees, and when the big man stood again he felled him with a left hook that almost broke his jaw. Standing over him, fingers slowly unclenching, he gulped at the air.

"You'll find a pistol in my room, Ben," he told the old man, who had sidled in to watch the fight with awed eyes. "Load and prime it. If this beast isn't gone when he's washed off the blood, put a ball between his eyes."

"Aye, sir. That I will, with pleasure!"

The girl was at his elbow then, a dirty hand reaching out to touch him fearfully. As he swung on her, she recoiled, blue eyes shading themselves behind long yellow lashes. She was a pretty thing, with a thick mass of blonde hair spilling across white shoulders, her hips straining the linsey-woolsey of her dress. Her features were grimed by a splash of dirt from ear to mouth and a smear of oil lay above her left eyebrow, but her mouth was ripe and red, and there was a creamy texture to her skin that made his eyes dip to the torn bodice where her breasts pressed their roundness into the homespun.

"Thank you, sir. Thank you for saving me from—from that."

He had seen camp trulls before. They followed the armies from camp to camp, and waited for the men, sometimes, within smelling distance of the cannons. This one was a cut or two above most of the wenches who knew the blackberry clumps and buttercup fields with such easy familiarity. Something inside him answered when she let him see her blue eyes fully, for the first time.

"I don't require your thanks." He smiled, staring at his torn sleeve and blood-spattered shirt. How could he ride to the Hall like this? He said almost unconsciously, "I did it for Ben, if you must know."

Her gasp told him he had been rude. He flushed and explained, "At first I did it for Ben, because he hit him. Then, later on—"

Her chin tilted. There was pride in those blue eyes, he was discovering. "Just the same, I thank you."

The big man stirred, groaning, and the girl trembled and stared down at him. She moved closer to Stafford, and now he could sense the fright in her. "He'll be after me again, soon's he comes to his senses. After you go, he'll get me." The girl put a grimy hand on his wrist. "Please, sir, could I go along with you, for just a little way?"

"I've only one horse. I'm sorry."

"I could ride behind you!" she pleaded eagerly. "I've done that before. Ridden behind a man on a horse, without a saddle under me."

"Yes, I rather suppose you have."

Stafford was staring at the big man on the floor, and so he did not see the deep-red flush that slid from her throat into her cheeks. He said reflectively, "He'll be vicious when he comes to. His kind always are, after a beating. Perhaps you'd best come with me, after all."

Her gaze was steady on his face. "You'd take a dog with you, to save him from a beating, wouldn't you?"

Stafford was surprised. "Why, I suppose I would. Yes."

For a moment, he thought she was about to slap him. Then she whirled on a heel and moved toward the door. For the first time, Stafford saw that she was barefoot. He wondered idly if she wore anything at all under that thin linsey-woolsey thing. He turned to Ben Leap.

"Get the pistol, Ben. Put it handy when he washes up."

"I will, sir. And—it's good to have you home again."

The girl was standing beside the stallion waiting for him, smoothing its nose with a palm, speaking to it in whispers. Grimy though she was, with a trace of the street urchin about her, the sunlight on her golden hair and face seemed to soften the dirt with an earthy honesty. Her slim white ankles made him curious as to the shape of the legs the green homespun skirt hid. His eyes traced her round hips and slim waist, and the firmness of her bosom.

When she felt his eyes on her, she slid away from the horse.

"Mount up," he told her gently. "I'll walk beside you."

"No," she whispered, letting him see the gratitude shining in her eyes. "No, I won't let you do that. I'd rather ride behind you."

Stafford put on his blue velvet jacket and studied himself. The coat would hide the tears in the shirt and the blood that flecked it. Then his toe jabbed the iron stirrup and he rose easily into the saddle. He bent and grasped the girl by her wrist and helped her swing behind him.

She straddled the stallion, skirt pulled to mid-thighs. As he turned back, Stafford reflected that the promise of her slim ankles was fulfilled in the shapeliness of the legs she bared by her action.

"Hold to me," he told her gruffly, and felt slim brown arms creep about his waist. A toe moved the horse into a canter.

They rode through the Virginia afternoon with the cry of a blue heron in their ears, with the scents of fall wildflowers growing in little bunches beside the dusty road touching their nostrils. The sunlight made a haze of the Carolinas to the south, and dappled the forestland stretching as far away as the mountains with golden splinters.

The girl was warm and soft behind him. His back was aware of her unbound breasts prodding it, and his waist tightened against the occasional tug of her young arms when the stallion broke stride to avoid a rut in the road. Once a thick yellow strand of hair brushed like a soft whip across his face, its perfume faint and disturbing. Against the back of his neck, he felt her soft breath.

She was a camp trull, though the most attractive one he had ever seen. If he wanted, he could turn the horse aside into the flanking forests that made this southern edge of Virginia a vast woodland and draw her down and enjoy her. She would not put up such a fight as she had with the big man in the ordinary. There was tenderness in the clinging of her arms around him, and a hidden hunger in the sudden hardening of the breasts on his back that told him she might even be eager for the caresses he could give.

Stafford thought of Laura Lee in the Hall, hoping she was waiting after four years to welcome him home, and put such thoughts from him. He urged the stallion to a faster pace.

When they came at last to the crossroads between the Dan road and the Carolina settlements, he turned in the saddle and smiled at her. "Where will you go now?"

"To Charlotte Town."

Charlotte Town. That was where Dan Morgan, recently made a brigadier general by the Continental Congress, was gathering the remnants of the army Horatio Gates had allowed the British to smash at Camden. A camp girl like this one, with her pert face and comely body, would find good pickings there. Men from the Maryland and Delaware regiments, mountaineers with their long Deckard rifles, and the army moving south with Nathaniel Greene would furnish her with an unlimited clientele.

She was very near. An arm hooked about her waist would crush her softness against him. Those full lips, pouting a little under his regard, would taste sweet to his starving mouth. As if sensing the hunger in him, she sat waiting, breathless, her blue eyes locked with his gaze. Four years is a long time, he told himself.

And then the moment was gone, and she was sliding groundward, her skirt lifting nearly to her hips. She paused on the ground, shaking out her dress, ignoring the fact that her bodice gaped where it had been torn. Her smile was bright as she raised her head, and he fancied that her blue eyes mocked him.

"I wish you luck, sir," she said softly. "All the very best of luck."

Then she was moving away, with the dust rising in little puffs about her bare feet, her hips twitching to each stride, the long yellow hair falling almost to the small of her back. Stafford stared after her, motionless, until she was gone out of sight around a bend in the road and under the sheltering branches of the towering pines.

He sighed and toed the stallion to a gallop. Eagerness beat in him with a rising pulse. Less than a dozen miles from here was Laura Lee, and home.

Ezra Whipple bent to the wash pan, sloshing cold well water onto his bruised face. Fire ate in him, a roaring flame of hate and frustration that called on his pride for vengeance. No man ever before had stood to the thud of his meaty fists. He had fought fair and foul more times than he could remember, with all manner of men. Once his thumbs had gouged the eyes from a Pennsylvania farmer. Once his teeth had chewed off the ear of a New York merchant in a Fly Market tavern.

He did not like the taste of his bruises. He toweled his face gently, aware that Ben Leap watched from the planked bar, a long-barreled horse pistol primed and cocked in his hand. The old man had taken the pistol from an upper room, from a room that belonged to the man who had beaten him so savagely.

"A good man, that one," he said grudgingly to Ben Leap, pretending affability. "At another time, I might have been his friend."

Ben Leap spat across the bar. "No friend of yours, you scum. He's a plantation man, a gentleman. The Staffords have been here in Virginia for near a century."

"Still and all, he's a man. A good man with his fists. He never let me get close enough to hug him once. If he had, I could have snapped the ribs of him like dry sticks. A good man."

"They come no better."

Whipple chuckled, and held his shirt aloft. "Tore it to tatters with his knuckles. Now where'll I get me another?"

Ben Leap eyed the big man curiously. He was an ordinary keeper, and his trade was buying and selling. He said slowly, "I could sell you one, for a shilling and tuppence."

The big man put a hand in his breeches pocket and brought out some coins. Placing them carefully on a table-top, he backed toward the stair. "Fetch me one. There's your money. I'll stay near the stair, to prove I mean you no harm."

Ben Leap reflected. The grip of the pistol in his hand

was reassuring. "I'll fetch one from the storeroom. No tricks, mind. I'd as leave shoot as not. I may be old, but I can use a firearm still."

Whipple laughed. "No tricks."

When the old man was gone, Whipple whirled and went up the stairs, three treads at a time. Impatiently he hunted, opening bedroom doors until he came to the room with the slanting ceiling and the dusty furniture. With the instincts of the burglar he once had been, in New York town before the war, he knew this for the room he sought.

On silent feet he went to the mahogany dresser, opening and closing drawers and finding them empty. He turned to the writing table, but abandoned that after a glance. His eyes touched the ironbound chest, slid away from it, and then returned.

He knelt. The lock was open. As his hands pushed up the chest top, he gasped. A hunting shirt and leggings, a carved powder horn marked with the Stafford name, a green sash and moccasins lay piled before him.

Wonderingly he lifted out the white buckskin hunting shirt. "One of Morgan's men! Ah, now why should he be so sly about the fact, unless he wants to keep it secret?"

Ezra Whipple knew the South was torn apart by strife between Tory and rebel. Fathers fought sons and daughters fought mothers. It might be that Colonel Billy Joe Stafford—the fringes on the hunting shirt told Whipple his rank—would be hurt by having his secret exposed.

The big man rolled the powder horn under the hunting shirt and tied them both with the green sash. His loose mouth twitched in a grin. Moving to the window, he tossed his little package out onto the grass of the side yard. He would cozen Ben Leap into telling him where the Stafford plantation was located. After that, he'd trust his ears and his tongue and his nimble wits to turn this secret to his advantage.

His fingertips touched the swollen bruises on jaw and cheeks. Billy Joe Stafford would pay for the beating he had given Ezra Whipple, in the way that would hurt him most.

Chapter Two

THE SIX white pillars of the Hall beckoned Stafford from three miles away. The rows of tall, shutter-hung windows, dimly seen in the shadows of the columned portico, were shy eyes peering out as if in disbelief at the sight of the master riding home at last. Sunlight glinted on the gambrel roof with its three great red-brick chimneys. Fresh paint gave the building an elegance that touched something deep inside him.

He let the stallion run along the graveled drive that curved by the outbuildings and the long white stables with their sweep of cypress shingles neat and spotless. Reining in with a scrape of gravel scratching sparks under iron horseshoes, he came out of the saddle with a call for the stables.

A black face framed in white hair was thrust above the half door of a stall. The eyes opened very wide and the mouth fell open. For a long instant Old Gem stared. Then his shaking hand was pushing aside the lower part of the door, and he was running forward, weeping in his delight.

"Master Billy! Master Billy!"

Stafford opened his arms wide and pulled the old slave into his hug. Then with his hands on the bowed shoulders he pushed the old man back and ran his eyes over him. "You look well fed, Gem! Something tells me that we aren't exactly starving at Stafford Hall these days."

A curious look touched the old slave's features. His eyes dropped as he said, "We eat good, Master Billy. We work hard, too. The mistress stands for no nonsense, 'cepting from—"

He broke off and fear showed in his old eyes. For a moment he hesitated, then straightened his shoulders. Old Gem knew what an angry master could do to a slave, but he was an old man, soon to die anyhow. For sixty years he had lived within sight of the Dan. He had seen the Hall grow from a little cabin to its present elegance. His hands had taught two generations of Staffords how to ride a

17

horse. Besides, this young giant before him loved him like a son his father.

"They's British officers always at the house, Master Billy. They bring gold for the wheat and vegetables we grow. The mistress has made you rich."

"On British gold," said Stafford, and he frowned.

Old Gem licked his lips. He said with a strange inflection in his voice, "One gennelman in particular. He's 'most always here. Right now, even."

He winced as powerful fingers dug deep into his arm. A hellish light began to glow in his master's eyes, a light that flared once and then died out to a still more frightening blankness.

Then Stafford was whirling and moving away, tall and powerful and somehow magnificent to the old slave, even in the old blue velvet frock coat and breeches that were too tight for him. Old Gem reached for the reins of the big stallion. His hard hands patted the sleek nose gently, but his eyes watched his master mount the stone steps of the portico and disappear between two tall white pillars.

"Never see the Stafford hell light in the young master's eyes before," he whispered to the horse. "Only in his daddy's eyes and in his granddaddy's eyes, when they were bent on killing a man."

Old Gem sighed and moved away, with the horse patiently trailing in answer to his tug on the rein.

The hall of the house was cool and white, with a high sheen on its mahogany butterfly table and matching chairs, as Stafford came through the doors. A gilt scroll-top mirror reflected the peacock design in the wallpaper and the glass base of the chandelier hanging on its chains from the high white ceiling.

Directly ahead was the wide, white door that led out to the herb garden. A spiral stairway twisted upward to the second story. Where the wide treads began, an open door spilled the sound of a teacup clinking against a saucer.

The thick hall carpeting caught the sound of his boots as Stafford moved toward the long parlor. He stood framed in the open doorway, seeing a tall Englishman in the red uniform jacket of a colonel of the Thirty-third Foot bowing before his wife, who sat with shoulders bared in the fashionable French cut of her gown, smiling up at him.

Laura Lee did not see him. The dark magnificence of a Chippendale highboy set between the garden windows framed her flushed face and its spirals of coiling brown hair. Moisture lay on her full red lips.

Remembrance of the hours they had spent in this room, and in the herb garden beyond the far windows, swept in a flood of weakness through Stafford. Laura Lee had come to Stafford Hall as a bride, young and ardent and curious, seven years ago. Time had matured her, put a gloss and a confidence in her manner, as it had added curving flesh to the body that the British officer was surveying as he sipped his tea.

"I vow and protest, Laury," he giggled, "you put a fever in my blood with your eternal teasings and cajolings. Promise me every dance this night. Promise me that."

With her ivory fan she touched his chin as he bent low above her. "La, sir. Such a fire in the man! I'll promise only the first and the last, to cool your fever."

"But later, when the ball is over? Ah, what then? Shall we—"

He broke off and straightened. Laura Lee was staring beyond him at the door, and there was something in her wide eyes that brought him around on a boot heel. The big man in the ill-fitting riding suit standing like a frozen giant in the doorway was staring at him with eyes that were strangely disturbing.

"Billy Joe! Oh, it can't be!" Laura Lee whispered, and put a trembling hand to the upholstered arm of the settee to rise to her slippered feet.

She swayed a little, and the Colonel took advantage of the fact to steady her by an arm about her waist. He growled, "Impertinent trespasser! Shall I throw him out on his ear, Laury?"

Her eyes touched his face a moment. "This is my husband, Colonel. Billy Joe Stafford, of Stafford Hall. Colonel Edmund Emerson."

"God's love!" Emerson whispered.

Stafford came forward to bow stiffly, a grim smile on his lips. Golden epaulets and a sword dangling from leather straps made Emerson seem a fine figure of a soldier to Stafford, who was used to the ragged Continentals and the buckskinned Marylanders and Virginians.

"I've been rude, Colonel," Stafford said. "I should have come with bugles blowing and heralds before me. Then I wouldn't have found you at such a loss." He swung to Laura Lee. "Four years is a long time, Laura. I can understand your state of shock. Shall we adjourn to the upstairs parlor?"

He was deliberately cold, almost aloof, but inside him he was fighting the same sort of seething madness that had taken his grandfather to his death on a dueling plot and sent his father racing off to two wars.

Laura Lee Stafford stared from the white lips of her husband to the florid countenance of the Colonel. Her smile was forced as she said, "Of course, darling! You'll excuse us, Colonel?"

The Colonel was profuse in his protestations of delight at being left alone. Stafford eyed the thin film of sweat on his forehead and smiled mirthlessly. He gave his elbow to Laura Lee, and noticed that the hand she rested on it trembled faintly.

With her painted satin skirts swishing crisply beside him, with her fragrance all around him, he led her to the doorway. As he turned, he saw the Colonel dabbling at his flushed face with a kerchief. Stafford bowed and closed the door.

Laura Lee took him up the spiraling staircase, wide hips swaying to each stride, past the paintings by Benjamin West and Sir Joshua Reynolds in their carved, gilded frames. Then the poplar planks of the upper floor were under their feet and she was pushing open the door to the upstairs parlor and moving into it.

Stafford followed, closing the door and putting his back to it. His eyes touched the smooth skin of her shoulders and strayed to the cleft of her bosom.

He sighed and said, "You've no idea how I looked forward to this home-coming, Laura. I pictured it to myself so many times. Each time it was different. Yet in all the different ways I pictured it, none mirrored the reality of your conduct with that lobsterback!"

Her ringed fingers clasped her little fan until the knuckles showed white ."Am I to be denied friends, even if they don't wear your precious Continental rags? You ran away, Billy. You left me all alone. I was never sure you'd come back."

His laughter was harsh. "Old Gem was sure. But then, Old Gem loves me."

She came forward three steps, until she stood close to him. Her eyes were dark and glowing beneath their long lashes. "You didn't run out on Old Gem! Ah, I waited. Waited and yearned for you to come back! But was I to bury myself like a nun in your absence? Don mourning clothes? I managed the plantation. I made new friends."

"The time must have gone very swiftly, in your amusements with His Majesty's officers!" He spoke out of the bitterness and the jealousy welling up inside him, born of the years of campfire dreams and the endless marches and retreats.

She came nearer, swaying easily, the smile on her moist red lips an intimate thing. Her body was soft and yielding as she pressed herself against him where he stood with his back to the white door. Tenderly she kissed his chin, standing on her toes. From his chin her mouth slid to the corner of his lips.

"Have you seen the house and outbuildings, the fields beyond them, dearest Billy? We have twenty more slaves and half a hundred more horses. And a fine new carriage. In the deepest part of the icehouse there are two chests buried. Each chest is filled with gold. I've been a good overseer in your absence."

Despite his anger and his hurt, she was a temptation to a man. Her breath was honey, and her stayless gown permitted him to feel the softness of her thighs and middle. She laughed and writhed lazily, lifting her bared arms to coil them about his neck.

"Are you supposing I've been unfaithful to you, Billy Joe? Do you accuse me in your mind of bundling with every officer in a red jacket that comes with payment for the goods I sell him? Is that what eats in your heart when it should be filled only with love for me?"

"Laura, Laura," he whispered, and moved his head so that her lips were grazing his. He shivered to their teasing while she whispered.

"We've a new bedroom suite," she told him, "done in mahogany by Thomas Chippendale of London town. You've never seen it, Billy Joe."

His palms were sliding up over her arms to her satiny shoulders, and down her back to the lacings of her French gown. Almost unconsciously his fingers worked at those laces, until the gown fell apart to the small of her back.

Dimly he was aware that she was choosing this method of making him her slave again, as she had done those years before, when she had come as a bride to the Hall. She had come a virgin to his big canopied bed, but she had brought her library with her, and such wisdom as she had culled from the pages of Ovid and Jean de la Fontaine and Restif de la Bretonne. Her desire to test that wisdom was as fierce as his anxiety to share it. With languor and with hungry sensuality they had learned together the arts of the flesh.

Her thin silken shift parted as he ripped it. Now her entire back was like creamy satin under his hands and fingers, as far down as her rounded hips. Moaning softly, she arched to him. A single movement of his hands would bring gown and panniers, modesty bit and Medici collar from her body, leaving her naked to his eyes.

"Billy Joe! It's been so long, so long!"

"Too long, Laura. Too long!"

What thought had he for the fact that she was a Tory and he a rebel? She was his wife, and he had not seen her for four years. She was in his arms now and quivering against him, pleading a little, with her wet lips to his ear, her own hands like hungry talons. Of this pressure of lips to lips and hands moving easily on soft flesh he had dreamed in camps from Quebec to Valley Forge. Now the opportunity was with him to turn those dreams to reality.

His cry was harsh and frantic as he brought his arms down, his hands filled with lace and satin. For an instant he paused, staring at the white body that was even more intoxicating than he remembered, and then he was lifting her and moving toward the bedroom suite that he had never seen.

The sweetish scent of bayberry candles, the clink of Stourbridge glassware, and the muted drone of conversation made Stafford drowsy. He lolled against the high back of his Elfe chair, aware that the officers of His Majesty's Thirty-third Foot, Thirty-seventh Foot, and Royal Welsh Fusileers were drinking his health and the health of his beautiful wife in rich red port. His buff and

purple coat and breeches, hurriedly altered and refitted
by a tailoress in from the slave cabins on the Dan, fitted
him exactly, so that he seemed a very Beau Nash for
elegance.

The war was far away. It was good to sit here, with the
candles guttering softly, with the wild turkey he had just
eaten and the varieties of wines he had quaffed in pleasant
toasts to the standards of the several British regiments
warm within him. He looked at Laura Lee, and smiled
contentedly. In the upper bedroom that long afternoon,
she had made his every dream a reality, draining him of
the hungers that had run in him for a seeming eternity.
He put his thoughts of the war behind him and reached
for the goblet that Old Gem was filling.

Over the rim of the goblet he caught Colonel Edmund
Emerson staring at him with savage intentness. He had
seen men who looked at him like that before, over the
muskets that King George III issued to his soldiers. Then
Emerson was glancing aside, and Stafford put the look
he imagined down to the jealousy that had burned in him
that afternoon.

A chair scraped. A scabbard clanked on its chains.
Golden epaulets caught the gleam of the table candles.
They were rising, these British officers and the women
they had brought with them from Winnsboro and from
Charles Town, to adjourn to the large ballroom across
the hall. The cadence of strings and spinnets was summoning them to the dancing.

"The first dance belongs to me, Laura Lee," he whispered.

"To no one else, my darling." She smiled, and the pressure of her fingers on his hand made his heart leap.

He went with her across the hall, the British officers
drawing back courteously. He did not see Colonel Emerson staring after him with slitted eyes, did not see him
turn on a heel and move toward the tall French windows
that opened onto the terrace and to the herb garden
beyond.

The nights were cool in November. Colonel Emerson
moved to the stone rail of the terrace and stared out over
the fall herbs and flowers in their patterned beds, biting
hard at his full lower lip.

"Milord!"

It was only a whisper in the night from the darkness below him, but it made the Colonel freeze. He put a hand to his belt, where his service pistol hung, as he leaned over the balustrade.

"Who's there? Eh? Who is it?"

"Ssssst! Not so loud, milord!"

A big man came out of the shadows, a bulky package in a hand. He was heavy-set, with uncut black hair and small, glittering eyes.

Emerson surveyed him, faint disdain curling his lips. "You want me, my man?"

"You're a Britisher, ain't you? A Britisher interested in capturin' a rebel posing as a loyalist and a man of property?"

There was something in the tone of the big man that caused the Colonel to glance at the French windows off the terrace. He went and closed them, then came back to the wide stone steps that ran down to the garden. A vague hope was blooming in him as he saw the big man kneeling and undoing the green sash with which he had tied his bundle.

Ezra Whipple spread the buckskin hunting shirt wide and laid the green sash on top of it. He held a powder horn carved almost to transparency in his hands, turning it over and over as his eyes caught at the Colonel.

Emerson gasped. "A rebel uniform. One of Morgan's sharpshooters!"

"Aye! The fringes mark it for a colonel's shirt, milord."

Colonel Emerson lowered his voice. "Who owns the thing, man?"

Cunning lay deep in Whipple's eyes. He shifted restlessly, and sighed. The beating he had taken that afternoon had put the thirst for vengeance in him, but not to such an extent that it removed the greed that was a perpetual fever in his blood.

Putting a hand to his pocket, Emerson drew out a velvet purse. As he hunkered down, he unfastened it and poured a flood of round golden sovereigns into his palm. Silently Ezra Whipple eyed that small fortune, licking dry lips with his tongue. Impulsively he held out his hand for the gold.

Colonel Emerson laughed softly. "Not so fast, not so

fast. How do I know it's worth my gold, this uniform you bring?"

Whipple scowled. His narrowed eyes studied the face of the British officer, reading the sensuality that lay in his too-full mouth, in his flushed cheeks and glittering eyes. For an hour he had lain on the flagging of the terrace, staring in at the diners. He had seen the manner in which this man's eyes roved the figure of the woman who sat at Stafford's elbow.

"Ye mind the man in the high splat-backed chair? The man who's wed to the dark beauty?"

Emerson gasped and hunched closer. "Stafford? God's my life! Can you mean Stafford?"

"Aye. Billy-Joe Stafford. One of Dan Morgan's colonels!"

Emerson came to his feet. He stood rigid, letting triumph sweep across him. Stafford a rebel! Stafford, now in gentleman garb, out of uniform! He could hang him out of hand, now, to the nearest tree!

As a man might savor old wine, so Colonel Emerson savored the thoughts he held. Now he would not be a trespasser in that big canopied bed above the ballroom. Now he could wed with Laura Lee, and own the plantation she governed. All these fine buildings, the slaves and horses, the meadows rich with wheat and cotton would be his! When the war was over, he would stay on in the colonies, perhaps helping to administer this rich territory of Virginia for the crown.

It was a magnificent prospect to a man who had been born out of wedlock to an English earl, to a man who had been trained for war at a military academy, who expected nothing other than his officer's pay and an occasional chance to loot a Southern plantation in return for his service.

He swept the gold and the purse into Whipple's hands. "Tell me how you came by them. Tell me what proof you have that they belong to him."

Ezra Whipple told him of the fight that afternoon, and of the blonde girl, and of the little room in the Black Thistle ordinary and the chest it held. Then he showed him the powder horn with its scrolled Stafford crest.

"It will be enough." Emerson laughed, and there was cruelty in the sound.

Whipple stood up and put the gold in a pocket. He said hoarsely, "Your worship may have need of me in later times. I'll not be far away."

Emerson looked at his grossness, at the pig eyes and hulking shoulders. He smiled faintly. "It may be as you say. Don't go far away." Then he swept up the green sash and the hunting shirt and the powder horn and paced lazily toward the deserted dining room.

They were moving in the stately steps of a minuet as he came through the archway of the ballroom, its glass chandeliers and candles blazing, the music washing across the officers in their scarlet jackets faced in blue and silver, and over the women with their arms and shoulders bared. The paneled walls were rich with pine wainscoting, and the dark, polished flooring was so bright that it caught and held the reflections of officers' boots and swinging panniered skirts.

He stood with the hunting shirt and sash in a hand, savoring the moment. Laura Lee moved easily with Stafford, laughing up at him, cajoling him as she was wont to cajole himself. A few moments from now those lovely brown eyes would be wide in terror. Stafford would be wrestling against the grip of a score of hands, being dragged outward to the nearest tree!

Laura Lee Stafford would be a widow soon. He would remain behind to comfort her, after the others were gone. The anticipation of that comforting was in him as he made his way to the musicians' dais.

The music ceased abruptly at the wave of his hand. In the silence, men and women turned toward him curiously. Colonel Emerson spread out the hunting shirt and sash on the spinnet.

"Colonel Stafford, I've just been handed your uniform. It marks you as an officer in Morgan's Rifles. I find you out of uniform at the moment." The Colonel paused, savoring the stunned shock on Stafford's face, the dismay in Laura Lee's white cheeks. He said lazily, "I presume you know the rules of war, and what happens to a spy when his enemy catches him?"

The gloating was clear in his voice. His hand lifted the powder horn and held it high above his head for all to see.

"Gentlemen: his powder horn, with the Stafford crest

worked into it! I ask your aid in hanging this man for a spy!"

There were some who cried out against such a return for Stafford hospitality, but the majority of officers had seen those expert riflemen of Dan Morgan's cut more than one command to pieces behind them, and so they surged forward now, crying out harshly, dragging at their swords with eager hands.

Stafford stood still, the shock of discovery paralyzing his muscles.

Laura Lee gasped beside him, her hand working tensely at his forearm, "Deny it, Billy Joe. Deny it! You can save yourself that way!"

He could not save himself. Something in the face of Colonel Edmund Emerson whispered that he would listen to no argument. Something also told Stafford that it was not because he was a rebel that the Colonel was so eager to hang him.

Stafford was aware that everything in his life was crystallizing at this moment. Like his father before him, he had been born on this side of the Atlantic, and the vast freedom of the pine forests and the distant blue mountains was in his blood. Against that love of liberty was balanced the love he gave his wife. Not to embarrass her, not to extend into a perpetual bitterness their sometimes angry quarrels over a supposed duty to George III, he had run away four years ago. Now his absence was explained; now all the world knew him for a rebel.

He was not ashamed of the truth. It was only that he hoped to protect Laura Lee. It came to Stafford in this instant of his exposure that he was somewhat symbolical of the entire South. The Southern colonies were torn with inner dissension between loyalty to the crown and rebellion. Father and son, nephew and uncle, cousin and cousin were on opposite sides. Even as his own family was being torn apart now, so other families, from the Georgia settlements to the Piedmont uplands of Virginia, were being sundered by this war.

The scrape of a sword blade coming out of its scabbard called him to his senses. Men were pressing forward. Hands came reaching out to grasp him.

Stafford moved like a panther.

His years of fighting and starving with Morgan had made a steel spring of his big body. One moment he was standing motionless, as if dazed with despair, then he was five feet away, gripping the arm of a captain and whirling him sideways off his feet, flinging him against the men who ringed him in.

He needed no weapon in his hand. There were too many men around him to swing a sword, even if he should yank one from a scabbard, and too many men for any of them to fire a pistol, for fear of dropping a fellow officer.

Women were screaming, fainting into the arms of their escorts, unconsciously aiding him as he drove for the garden windows. Majors and captains must pause and attend to the women who fell into their open arms. More than half the others were unaware of what was taking place until after Stafford hit the tall, glass-set doors and was through them and out onto the terrace flaggings.

The night air was cool on his face. He put a hand to the rail and vaulted it, and angled his run toward the big white stables. He did not see Ezra Whipple come up out of the shadows with a musket at his shoulder and take aim.

Stafford was diving for the darkness of the stables as the musket blazed. The ball caught his jacket at the shoulder and tore a hole in it. If the light had been more even, and Stafford a little slower of foot, the ball would have caught him in the forehead, where it had been aimed.

Old Gem came out of a stall, leading a big black gelding.

"Here, Master Billy! The fastest thing on four legs we own!"

"Good, Gem! How'd you know?"

Old Gem smiled, showing glistening white teeth. "I hear the noise. I see you come out the door. I can saddle a horse in the dark, real quick."

The stirrup was underfoot, taking his weight, and then his leg was going over the saddle and he came down hard into the saddle. The other end of the stable was open to the meadow. Gem cried out, and Stafford heard his old palm hit the gelding as his own toes rammed its sleek black sides.

The gelding erupted into full gallop. Head bent, Stafford went out the west door, riding low. Behind him were the hoarse yells and outcries of angry men. A voice was shouting into the stable, but Old Gem would be fading to invisibility, through the roofed arcade that joined the stable with the carriage barn. In a few minutes the old slave would be tucked in his bed, stupid with sleep when they came to question him.

Stafford rode at breakneck speed for a mile, then swung the gelding southward into the pine barrens that ranged for miles beside the Dan. No man living could find him in these barrens. Stumbling Bear, a Cherokee brave who had met his death with Cornstalk in the Ohio country in '77, had taught him woodlore in his youth. Sometimes a group of Carolinians, on their way to Boonesboro and the blue-grass country of Kentucky, stopped overnight at the big Stafford plantation. Those men had added their own wisdom to the canny teachings of the Cherokee.

Finding a branch tipped with foliage, Stafford broke it off close to the bole and used it as a drag along the ground behind him. Switching it back and forth, making it seem some grotesque tail that waggled as the horse walked, he obliterated his hoofprints in the sandy soil.

The rhythmic sway of the horse as he walked put a bemusement in Stafford. Behind him, a part of his life was ending. No longer would he chase a giggling, teasing Laura Lee through the upper rooms of the Hall, to catch and subdue her breathless with kisses. Never again would they ride side by side across the meadows to survey the ripening wheat and the little white puffs of budding cotton. The disunity between them, which they had tried to ignore as long as it was secret, was now an open sore.

Laura Lee was a loyalist. He was a rebel. From the agony of spirit inside him, he knew at last the wrenching fury that was splitting his Southland. For his country, because of this wild hope for freedom that was inside him, he was giving up his wife and all his wealth.

When he was five miles into the barrens, he dismounted beside a little stream and sat a while, brooding at the water as it gurgled over the pebbles and between fallen pine branches. The scent of forest underbrush was strong around him, and somewhere a wolf howled its hunger.

"It isn't the wealth I mind losing," he told the brook, "but Laura Lee."

Yet Laura Lee was as determined in her way as he was in his own. She had called him traitor and turncoat when he first broached the idea that she go North, as so many Southern women were doing, at the start of the revolution. Fiercely she had challenged him, using tears and sobs to distract him from his beliefs. Finally, almost in desperation that last night, she had used her body.

A wry grin twisted his mouth as he remembered that night. He groaned and struck a fist to his knee. "If only I could convince her I was right! If only I could change her mind! She could live like a queen on those little chests of gold in the icehouse. She wouldn't want for a thing! Just so I could get her North, in Philadelphia or Boston, away from these British officers who bedazzle her eyes with visions of society!"

And what sort of man could he call himself, an inner voice asked, if he gave up now, and rode off like a beaten creature? One last try, one last and final argument! He was her husband. Once she loved him deeply. Perhaps she loved him still. He came to his feet eagerly, a pulse of excitement making him shiver. She had been wanton with him short hours ago, welcoming home her husband as a loving wife should do. Were those sighs and soft moans only acting? If she loved him as much as it seemed, she might be willing to listen to him at last.

"No, by God!" he breathed through his teeth. "She couldn't have been play-acting! She loves me! She told me as much today! Since she loves me so, she'll do as I say, to please me!"

He laughed, and there was no memory of their former quarrels in that laughter. Like a boy he went to the gelding, talking in careless fashion to the big black horse, rising easily into the saddle. Sweep her off her feet! Give her no chance to refuse! Make her agree! Then bring her with him, stirrup to stirrup at a mad gallop for Charlotte Town, where Dan Morgan was gathering his men.

She can go North under the protection of Old Gem and some younger slaves, he thought. I'll hire rifles to go with her, if need be.

As he rode he hypnotized himself with delusions that were born of his desperate need for affection and belief after the years of starvation and loneliness. He rode flushed and confident in his eagerness.

It was long after midnight when he came in sight of the Hall and its six towering white columns. The gigs and carriages were gone from the drive. Only the moonlight on white columns and Flemish brickwork relieved the darkness of the house. Quietly he walked the black across the grasses of the yard, until, by mounting onto the saddle, he could reach up and grasp the lowest crossbar of the latticework bordering the west wall. There was no sign that there were British soldiers still about, but he took no chances.

He pulled himself upward, foot by foot. The house was silent, dark, seemingly deserted. Now the middle bar was under his shoes, now the topmost.

A hand fumbled to find the window open against the autumn air. Then his leg swung over the white sill and he was halfway into the bedroom when he heard a voice cry out hoarsely.

A man and woman sat up in the bed where he had lain that afternoon. The woman was Laura Lee, with the moonlight silvering her body. She came out of the bed to stand staring at him.

"You fool!" she cried out hoarsely. "You poor, misguided fool!"

Then she was turning and running for the door, reaching out for its iron knob. The man who had been with her in the bed stood up now, and Stafford saw that it was Colonel Emerson. His right hand held a pistol that he had snatched from a little bedside table, and he trained it on Stafford, an inch above his belt buckle. The Colonel said triumphantly, "I told you he'd be back, Laury! I win our little bet! Now unbolt the door and summon the guards I posted below."

"Laura Lee! As you love me, leave the door alone!"

He was not aware that he cried out so, with the bitterness alive in him and the numb shock and disbelief raging. Behind him his hand fumbled, and his fingers closed on a covered compote glass. Even as his grip hefted it, he remembered the day he and Laura Lee had bought it in a Charles Town chinaware shop.

Then he was darting sideways and hurling the glass, seeing the cover fly off as it hurtled across the room. Startled, Colonel Emerson fired. A spit of flame ran at Stafford. He heard the ball whistle past and shatter a window glass be-

hind him. Then he was lunging forward, following the
glass, taking Emerson about the knees and hurling him
backward onto the bed.

Stafford was a madman for a few minutes. The hell light
in his eyes was alive and leaping, and the frenzy rose up
into his throat, shaking him with its power.

His fists thudded home on jaw and belly. He rode the
man's middle, hunting for his throat with hard hands. As
his fingers tightened on that throat, the door opened and
a shaft of yellow candlelight from a wall sconce came in
and showed him the purpling face, the bulging eyes and
protruding tongue.

Laura Lee was screaming at the doorway.

Heavy feet were pounding up the spiral staircase. Men
were shouting, and the noise of their shouting was growing louder.

Remembering her nakedness, Laura Lee ran to a chest of
drawers, snatched up a thin night robe, and slipped her
arms into it. As if that were a signal, red-jacketed soldiers
of the Thirty-third Foot came swarming through the door
and raced for the men grappling on the bed.

Stafford whirled back to sanity as a rifle butt came
stabbing through the pool of yellow candlelight at him.
He rolled from the musket, taking the man who held it
in the middle with a hard fist. As the man fell, Stafford
shoved him sideways and dived for the open window.

Beyond the window was a big cypress. He bunched his
legs under him and aimed for the branches. Then the
air was cold on his face and the tree was coming nearer and
there was nothing between him and the ground, thirty
feet below. His hands went out and closed on bark. He
slipped and slid, and then his hands caught purchase.

A musket spat at him from the bedroom window. Another musket joined it. He heard the balls bury themselves
in the tree bole.

A numbness of spirit made him cling there, with his
back offering a splendid target for the British soldiers. In
this moment of stark heartbreak and agonized despair, he
did not care whether he lived or died. What he had seen
in that big bed as he came through the window, the contorted positions of Laura Lee and the British colonel, had
put a disease in his brain.

He wanted to die, hanging here, with a branch under

a leg and bark cutting into his palms. What reason had
he to fight for life? What did life hold out to him now?
His former love for Laura Lee, which was all that
had been left to him after the earlier happenings of the
night, was a bitter taste in his mouth. Let her have her
British colonel, if she wanted him so badly! By dying
here, he could give her that much.

The thought of the Colonel did what nothing else could
do. It turned the bitterness in him to anger, and the anger
into a need for vengeance. Live! his mind cried out to him.
Live so that you can make them pay for this moment! As
another musket ball grazed his cheek, he swung down
and to the far side of the great tree bole. Feet feeling for
branch crotches, he went down. Ten feet from the ground,
he jumped.

The gelding sidled nervously as he came at him. Scorning
the stirrups, he went up over his rump in a hand-propelled
leap. As his weight settled hard in the saddle, the big
black lunged forward into full gallop. For the second time
that night, Billy Joe Stafford rode away from his family
home with death only half a step behind him, with musket
balls whistling in the air and a curious deadness settling
in his middle.

Chapter Three

IT WAS five hours past dawn when Stafford came out onto the rutted path that ran for most of the 130 miles between the Dan River and Charlotte Town. The despair and madness that had been in him as he had ridden from Stafford Hall was changed now to a bitter, furious anger. His memories of Laura Lee were ashes in his mouth. More than once he had winced, deep inside him, when some unbidden recollection of her sensual frenzies had come welling up from forgetfulness to taunt him. Now it was Colonel Emerson who knew that sweet wantonness, those frenzied cajolings of which she was capable.

His hand had tightened again and again on the curving cherrywood stock of the long horse pistol at his pommel, the temptation strong within him to go back and put a ball between the Colonel's eyes, no matter what his soldiers would do to him.

"There's little profit for a man in madness, though," he told the wind in his teeth, and let the pistol go.

Mile after mile, the pounding hoofs of the gelding forged the bitterness in him to a hard, desperate savagery. In that mood he rode through the dawn, not seeing the woods awake to life about him. He galloped furiously, enjoying the hate and the need for vengeance that battened on the injured pride of him.

Ten miles deep into the pine forest, he came upon the British soldiers. There were three of them, foot soldiers from the Thirty-seventh Regiment, to judge from the numerals worked into the tall peaks of their black leather caps.

They did not hear him until he was almost on top of them, the loosely packed dirt muffling the thud of his horse's hoofs. The pistol came leaping up into his hand and his toes went digging into the gelding's ribs.

Exultation rode with Stafford as he rose in the stirrups. These were British soldiers, lobsterbacks. One of their own kind, who wore the same red across his shoulders, had bedded his wife this past night. Of a sudden, the war took on a more personal meaning to Billy Joe Stafford. He hurtled into the soldiers, not as a colonel of that

34

company of gentleman sharpshooters, Morgan's Rifles, but as an aggrieved husband.

The pistol belched and an infantryman crumpled side-wise into a cranberry thicket bordering the road. Then the gelding was on the remaining men, hitting them into each other with his glossy shoulder, driven by powerfully thrusting legs. The pistol barrel flashed in the morning sunlight as it came whipping down across a man's temple.

He fought with a wild insanity, his pistol flailing and his eyes rolling. His pale-yellow hair, worn long, as was the custom, came free from the rawhide tie that held it in a bun at his neck. His torn shirt, ripped by thorns and brambles in his wild night riding, flapped from his ribs and arms. He saw these British regulars, not as enemy soldiers, but as kin to the man who had betrayed his home.

He overrode them with his fury, and as the third man crumpled across the road he reined in, sorry that the moment was over.

It was then that half a dozen heads came poking up from the bushes bordering the road, white faces peering at him from under the tall black caps with their chains and GR worked into the peaks. Terror showed in their white eyes. They were certain that he had an army at his back, as they wheeled and fled.

Stafford came down out of the saddle, running to the man sprawled in the roadway, lifting his powder horn and shaking a charge of the glossy powder into his pistol barrel. With a grim smile on his lips, he guessed at something of the successes of the man they named the "swamp fox," Francis Marion. The British swore a thousand men trailed him on his night rides. Stafford knew that he rarely had more than twenty at his back.

He moved from the fallen soldier to the gelding. As he was settling a toe in the iron stirrup, he heard a subdued groan. Turning aside, he parted the branches of a wild ginger thicket and stared.

A blonde girl lay at the base of a big oak tree, her wrists lashed tight behind her back. Her feet were bare, and her face was even more dirty than it had been at the Black Thistle ordinary when he had fought for her. Stafford chuckled and moved forward.

"So it's a prize I've won myself," he said to the girl,

aware that her gown was torn in such a fashion that all
of one white shoulder lay exposed to his gaze. "It's twice
I've saved you, so to speak."

Kneeling to free her wrists, he remembered Laura Lee,
and suddenly hated all women with a dark, wild hatred.
His hand tangled itself in her thick yellow hair and he
jerked her head back so that he could stare down into
her wide blue eyes. "What's to keep me from taking you
as a real prize, this time? You'd be a cuddly armful in an
ordinary bed. Pretty, too, with that filth washed off your
face."

His hand moved to her torn dress and lost itself inside
the homespun, caressing her until her face went scarlet.
"A nice, exciting shape to your body, as well. Ah, yes. We
can get along, you and I."

Stafford spoke in anger, but emotion had dined well
within him this last night and had left him weak. Too
weak to resist the surge that swept across him, born of the
softness and the prettiness of this lone blonde girl. His
arms lifted her and brought her against him, and he kissed
her hard and savagely.

She fought a little, but her mouth was moist fire and
it held Stafford by its very softness. He kept her submis-
sive to his caress for minutes, running his mouth from
her lips to her ear and then down to her soft throat. He
whispered hotly, "It's a colonel I am, with Morgan, and
with a colonel's privileges. You'll be no camp doxy, but
mine to care for and mine to protect from the camp filth
that will seek your cot of nights. Aye! I'll guard you better
than I guarded Laura Lee. I'll pay you, too. That's what
you want, isn't it? Good pay?"

She tried to struggle, straining back, held helpless both
by his strong arms and by the ropes still knotted about
her wrists, but when she realized that her convulsive writh-
ings served only to press her more tightly against him, she
went limp and unresisting.

When he let her go, her eyes were very steady.

"Untie my wrists," she whispered, her cheeks a flaming
red.

His face hard, he did as she asked him. When the
rope came free in his fingers, he put a hand to her wrist
and brought her to her bare feet. Bending to brush at
the twigs and fallen leaves that clung to her linsey-woolsey

dress, she ignored the fact that her bodice was gaping wide, and that his eyes were intent on the breasts that swung gently to her movements.

His hand still held her by a slender wrist. Gently she tugged her arm from his grasp and set her dress to rights. As she worked, she asked, "Who is Laura Lee?"

"A woman who calls herself my wife, who beds with any British officer who can bring her gold to put away against the gowns and carriages she wants to buy." He sneered. "You women! Grasping, greedy, all of you. You've only one thing to sell, but you drive hard bargains for it!"

Lazily she reached up and went to work on her yellow hair, attempting to free it of the tangles and the burrs worked into it. She said curiously, "Then she's no better than I am, is she?"

"Her price is higher," he told her bluntly.

She shrugged and smiled a little. It was a curious smile, and Stafford wondered for the moment what inspired it. When her hair was coiled so that it was free of her face, she said, "I've never been a private doxy before. It might be enjoyable, belonging to a man. To one man, that is. And I won't cost you so much. Certainly not as much as this Laura Lee!"

Mischief lay in her eyes. Suddenly her strong young arms were flung about his neck and she was pressing tight against him, her lips soft and open on his own. He drew back instinctively, and when he felt her shaking, he knew that she was laughing at him.

"You don't like to be overpowered, either, do you, Colonel? How do you think I felt, tied up and kissed like —like a—"

She moved away, extending her arms and twirling lightly around on her small bare feet. "Twice you've saved me. That should give you some claim to my—my services. Very well. I'll be your trull. It's a prospect I find not too displeasing, considering what a gentleman you are. Do you like what you're buying?"

Stafford found himself ill at ease. The anger and the savagery that had made him crush her in his arms had been a rebellion against the forces seething in him this past night. Now his wildness was gone, and shame lay in him. Stiffly he tried to apologize.

"La, there's no need for that," she told him. "I'm your

woman now. You won me twice. Once from that hairy beast, again from the British soldiers." With her skirt in her fingers, she danced toward him. "It's a bargain you'll have no cause to regret. I can be silent when you want silence, a very goose when you want chatter, and warm and ardent when you need comforting."

She came close, and it was Stafford that backed away. Then she giggled, and he laughed a little in response. "I'm Debby. Deborah Treat."

"Colonel Stafford, ma'am. Colonel Billy Joe Stafford."

He bowed gravely as she curtsied. There was a grace to her body and an elegance to the tilt of her blonde head that made him frown a little. She looked like no ·doxy that he had ever seen before. Most of them were blowzy, overfleshed women with dank hair and perpetual whines, always in dirty clothes and with dirt seemingly ingrained in their skin. This one had only surface dirt on her face and feet and arms, and her linsey-woolsey was worn and thin, but neat and only a little dusty.

He said, "The English may be back. It's best we take thought on our situation. I've some recollection of the fact that you're going to Charlotte Town."

Debby nodded pertly. "Where General Morgan is gathering what Gates left of his army at Camden. General Washington has named Nathaniel Greene to take over Gates's command."

The theatre of war was swinging southward in this autumn of 1780. Unable to bring their campaigns to a successful conclusion, the English turned their eyes to the Southern colonies. General William Howe, too concerned with his Mrs. Loring to be concerned with General George Washington, had allowed the Americans to winter out '77 at Valley Forge. His successor in command, Sir Henry Clinton, was eager but cautious.

Sporadic thrusts by the rebels at Canada in '75, the Cherry Valley fights with the Iroquois and Butler's Rangers against General Nicholas Herkimer, had taught the British respect for the ragged fanatics who never knew when they were beaten. Though they had won tactical victories at Brandywine and Germantown, Washington had come close to cutting the British army in two and capturing one half of it at Monmouth, in June of 1778.

Now the French were allying themselves with the colonists, and Sir Henry Clinton, who had almost lost his chestnuts at Monmouth against Washington, pulled back into New York. There was a good chance to snatch victory from the inconclusiveness of Monmouth by sundering Virginia and the Carolinas and Georgia from their Northern neighbors.

In accordance with this plan, Sir Henry Clinton and Charles Cornwallis came down on Charleston in the spring of 1780. When General Benjamin Lincoln surrendered to them, they spread out into the Carolinas.

Sir Henry Cinton turned the command in the South over to Cornwallis and went back to New York. With Sir Banastre Tarleton and his light cavalry in their green coats ravaging at will and earning themselves the hate of all Southerners by reason of their mercilessness, Cornwallis was free to move his forces where he willed.

To stop Cornwallis, Washington chose General Nathaniel Greene. Unfortunately, the Continental Congress refused to ratify this choice and sent Horatio Gates instead. Cornwallis caught Gates at Camden and whipped him thoroughly.

Now there was no American army in the South at all, except for a few mountaineers with long Deckard rifles, backed by a small detail of Morgan's Rifles under Colonel Stafford. With McDowell and Shelby and the backwoodsmen from the Carolinas, these sharpshooters caught Major Patrick Ferguson, who formed Cornwallis' left wing with his Rifle Corps, and shot his men to ribbons at King's Mountain.

A panicky Continental Congress deferred to General George Washington, and selected Nathaniel Greene as commander of the dispersed Southern army. They made Dan Morgan a brigadier general and sent him down to whip together the remnants of the army Gates had lost.

Billy Joe Stafford was riding now to rejoin Morgan, having already sent his detail of rifles on to Charlotte Town, his recent leave a bitter taste in his mouth. Reflecting on this, he turned from the girl and brought the gelding to her.

He mounted and swung her up behind him and they rode as they had ridden yesterday, with her arms about him and her softness pressed to his back. There was close to a hundred miles of swamp and canebrake country to

be traveled before they sighted Sugar Creek and the
gold mines sprawled eastward of Charlotte. Most of the
journey was through red-clay country below the Yadkin
River. For a while they followed the Great Trading Path,
which ran across the trading ford of the Yadkin and moved
through Salisbury southwestward, becoming the old War-
rior's Path running down to Charlotte.

Stafford skirted the main road on the chance that
some of Tarleton's men were out, burning houses and
barns and shooting rebels where they found them. He
kept to the ridge roads, twisting through a country of
deep ravines and sandy hillocks. The black was carrying
double, and he had no urge to press him, and so they
went lazily, with the days warm and the nights brisk with
November cold.

They came into Charlotte not far from the red-brick
meetinghouse, seeing the tents of the army that Dan Morgan was gathering from the mountains and the swamplands for Nathaniel Greene. Stafford swung the gelding
for the pole from which flew the flag of the Eleventh
Virginia Rifle Corps, with the numerals 1776 wreathed
above its lettering. They paced between veterans of Quebec and Saratoga, men who lifted bronzed faces with grins
of recognition for Stafford and low whistles of admiration for the girl. They paused in the mending of shot car-
touches and powder-horn thongs to stare and comment.

"They envy me," Stafford said wryly.

Debby arched closer to him so that she could whisper in
his ear. "They have no cause for envy. I can tell the
world you behaved like the gentleman you are."

He flushed, and at his flush she laughed softly.

"Would you have had me otherwise?" he growled.

She made no reply, but put her blonde head on his
shoulder and rode drowsily like that through the encampment, letting the men suspect what they would, aware
that Stafford was rigid with embarrassment.

When he swung her to the ground before the large
tent where General Morgan kept his headquarters, his
eyes were bright. "When I've finished my business with
Dan, I'll find us a room in the town. There we can make
good the affectionate promise you showed my men."

She laughed and turned on a heel, making for the open
tent flaps. He followed her bare heels into the tent.

Dan Morgan was deep in parchment maps and sheaves of papers at the crude planking that served him as a desk. When his eyes made out Stafford in his frilled lawn shirt and velvet breeches, he grinned and leaned back in the splat-backed chair his men had requisitioned from a town house.

"Billy Joe! I heard you and Shelby and McDowell gave Ferguson his come-uppance at King's Mountain."

"The ,boys were shooting well, Dan. That checked shirt the Scotchman wore made a fine target for our shot."

Morgan looked at Deborah Treat, and amusement lay deep in his gaze. He was a big man, powerful and fleshy. He had fought with Braddock when the French had smashed him at Fort Duquesne, and had volunteered his services and those of his rifles to Washington at Cambridge at the outbreak of the Revolution. He had lost none of his energy, despite his capture* at Quebec and subsequent service at Saratoga and in Washington's campaigns, following his return to duty after a prisoner exchange. It was his custom to recruit men with his fists, but the Bible that lay amid the papers on the desk planking showed him also to be a man of deep religious vein.

He said gruffly, "I see you've brought along a recruit for the corps. Can she shoot?"

Debby smiled and put a hand to her neck, bringing out a small golden chain that held a locket whose face was fitted with an onyx glory hand. Lifting it off her neck, she held it out to Morgan.

The sight of that glory hand brought Morgan to his feet. His fingers shook as he extended them for the trinket.

"The glory hand that Washington promised!" His hard eyes lifted to the girl. "You'll be no common camp girl. You must be—"

Deborah glanced mischievously at a staring Stafford, lips curving into a gentle smile. "Mistress Deborah Treat, General. Of the Roanoke Valley Treats."

Stafford started. He had known the Treats in those forgotten years before the war. Alexander Treat had been a hothead, as he remembered him. Complaining bitterly of the Stamp Act of '65 and of the Townshend Acts of '67, he remained completely unappeased when they were repealed. Savage at the treatment of colonial planters by

London merchants and their agents, the old man had advised rebellion even before Sam Adams painted his cheeks red for his Boston tea party. He had not known that the old fire-eater boasted such a daughter.

The remembrance that he had considered her a doxy gnawed in him. Her family was as long in Virginia as his own. The mansion Alexander Treat had built was a heap of burned cinders now and his possessions were scattered to the winds, but his blood still ran hot in the shapely limbs of this girl.

"My apologies," he muttered stiffly.

"La, Colonel Stafford," she replied merrily, "your conduct was a compliment to my disguise!"

She went on to tell Morgan that General Washington had advised secret travel, rather than in a carriage by the post roads from Philadelphia to Fredericksburg and south to Hillsboro. Dan Morgan grinned hugely as she related how Stafford had put blue bruises on Ezra Whipple's cheeks, and how his single pistol had overcome the British regulars who had captured her five miles beyond the Dan.

"A good man with his fists and a gun, Billy Joe," admitted Morgan, "but something remiss when he has aught to do with women. They terrify him."

"I had not noticed," she answered innocently, then flushed red when Morgan whooped his laughter.

As he wiped his eyes, Dan Morgan looked from his colonel to the blushing girl. "Forgive my levity. God knows we rebels get few enough chances for laughter these black days. It's welcome you are, Mistress Treat. I'll make some arrangement with Mrs. Pickens in town for your boarding."

"Am I to remain here long, sir? I'd thought there was some haste to my mission."

"And so there is. But we've certain steps to take before that mission can do us any good. I've been in postal touch with General Greene, and have shared his confidences to some extent. He arrives at Charlotte within a week or two, after meeting Gates at Hillsboro."

Morgan paused and puckered his lips, frowning thoughtfully. "We don't have much of an army to oppose Cornwallis. We smashed his left wing under Ferguson at King's Mountain, but he still has close to fourteen thousand men under his command. We have less than three thousand. And still, Nat has some wild notion of splitting our small forces in half!" He paused and stared at the hard-packed dirt floor of his tent. "It's suicide. Either suicide or—military genius."

Morgan grinned infectiously. "Nat and I like to think it's genius. We can't beat Charley Cornwallis in a mixed battle, but we might take a poke at him if we can get him to split up his own command. Before we can do that, we have to know what his plans of attack are, and what hell he's likely to give us if we divide our forces."

Idly, Morgan put out a hand and ran his fingertips along the cracked binding of his Bible. "I've nobody I can fully trust, Billy Joe, except my own men. I'd like to send someone into Winnsboro, where Lord Charley makes his headquarters, to discover that intelligence for me."

Stafford grimaced. "I've little stomach for spying."

Morgan nodded sourly. "I remember what we did to André, and what the lobsterbacks did to Nathan Hale. I'd never ask a man to do a job I dislike myself, but necessity forces it on me. We might have a chance, if we can get Cornwallis to send that hellbound Tarleton after one part of our army. Otherwise—"

The General shrugged and went around the end of his plank desk to sit down. His hands came together, his fingers locking. When Deborah Treat spoke sharply, he glanced curiously at her thoughtful face.

"I have business in Winnsboro myself, General Morgan. It may be that Colonel Stafford and I may go together."

"As brother and sister," said Morgan with a smile, "or even as husband and wife."

Debby laughed, and then sobered. "General Washington intimated that I was to have a free hand in my mission. If Colonel Stafford will aid me in my quest, I'll be only too happy to become another Peggy Shippen."

"We'll be obvious as cats in a cracker barrel," Stafford growled. "We'll need clothes and a carriage, if we're to pose as Tories enriched by their friendship with the British. Rich clothes. Elegant gowns. Sleek horses. If we were closer to the Dan, I'd get all that by robbing my own plantation. But down here—"

Morgan chuckled. "That's why I picked you for the job, Billy Joe. You're the only man in my command with

the social background to move in plantation society as
an equal. You know what you'll need and how to act."
He turned to Debby and bowed slightly. "You, too, Mistress Treat, are at ease in such company. It's the will
of the Lord you came at a time like this, when our need
is so great."

Stafford said, "What about the clothes? The horses
and carriage?"

"All taken care of. Marion's been out with his men,
looking for what I need. So has Sumter. We've a dozen
chests filled to their hasps with gowns and furbelows,
fans and shawls and petticoats for Mistress Treat and
fashionable garments for yourself. Quality clothes. I can't
wear 'em myself, but I know 'em when I see 'em!"

"When do you want us to ride?"

"At once. I can't wait until Nat gets here. I know his
mind, and he knows mine. We've worked together, under
Washington, before this. Get that information for me and
I'll see that Nat knows about it. Rest today. Leave tomorrow morning at sunup."

Mistress Treat curtsied. "Until then, General, I'll ap-
preciate your offer of a town house and bed. I haven't
slept properly in over a fortnight."

General Morgan pursed his lips and glanced at Stafford. Mistress Treat caught the glance and smiled sweetly.
"Colonel Stafford has been like a brother to me, General. I
consider it a good omen for our coming jaunt."

With her fingertips on Stafford's arm, she let him escort
her from the tent.

Colonel Edmund Emerson flicked an imaginary mote of
dust from the blue velvet cuff of his scarlet and gold uniform jacket. The bruises Billy Joe Stafford had put on
his throat a week before were still in evidence, and a spate
of fury shook him when he remembered the ignoble position he had played, flat on his back, clobbered by fists
and choked by hands in front of Laura Lee Stafford and
his own men.

"It's not to be endured," he told himself for the thou-
sandth time, touching the bluish mark on his cheek with
tender fingertips. "I'll seek him out and pay him back in
hot leads for the marks he's left on me. Stab me Satan,
but I will!"

The thought that a pistol ball in Stafford would make his wife a widow was comforting to the Colonel. It mollified the rage in him, until he could turn and preen himself before the upright Queen Anne mirror on the bedroom wall with something approaching his usual complacency.

He made a fine figure of a man, he admitted, eying his reflection. His red cloth coat had been made to order in London, its buff facings and gold lace on a dark-blue velvet background enhancing its elegance. His breeches of tight white drill showed off the muscular shape of his powerful legs, while the white stockings and shoes of black leather fitted with silver buckles added to the satisfaction with which he stared back at himself.

With a hand he slapped his belly. "No flab there! No wonder Laury's so taken with me." From a contemplation of his own figure, his eye turned inward to a mental contemplation of Laura Lee's loveliness. No woman he had ever known, from the Vauxhall Gardens in London to the dancing assemblies he had attended in New York and in Charles Town, ever had acted as such a catalyst to his emotions.

In Mrs. Stafford he discovered a sensuality to outdo his own desires. Her voluminous readings of Ovid and Boccaccio, her possession of such works as an unexpurgated edition of Lucian's *Golden Ass,* with properly impudicitic illustrations, *Pills to Purge Melancholy,* and Matthew Prior's poems made her section of the Stafford library a delight in which to browse.

The fact that Laura Lee enjoyed a practical application of her literary tastes made him her slave. Never before jealous of a woman, he was discovering in himself a reluctance to share her fleshly wisdom even with her legal spouse.

And so his trigger finger itched in rhythm with his steps as he went to find Laura Lee and acquaint her with the news that he would accompany her to Winnsboro. He discovered her in the study behind the spiral stairs, at a mahogany writing desk.

"An officers' ball, dearest Laury, to celebrate the whipping that Lord Cornwallis is preparing for Greene and Morgan," he told her, bowing over her hand. "We can stay the week at the King's Head ordinary."

Her dark eyebrows raised. "That would be a proper scandal, indeed. Even if Billy Joe is a rebel colonel, he's still my husband."

"But not for long. Someday soon I'll come on him and repay him for what he did to my face and throat."

"Poor Billy," she sighed. "He's such an idealist. He conceives sacrifice to be self-rewarding. He'd have had me residing at the London Coffee House in Philadelphia for the past five years, if I had let him."

"He'd have buried beauty and brains together, if he'd done that."

"Flatterer! Now leave me, Edmund, while I finish the accounts. We ship to Charles Town port this week end. I must have matters ready for Mr. Andrews, who handles my affairs there."

"The officers' ball, Laury? What of the ball?"

She reflected, staring across the room at the candle box hanging on the pine-paneled wall beside the bookshelves. She studied the damask curtains and design of the thick Turkish rug that had been imported during Billy Joe's youth. It came to Laura Lee that she was tired to death of this big house, and of the cares it brought daily to her little study desk.

In the oak chest in her bedroom she had new gowns from London stylists that she had never worn. They had come in exchange for the hogsheads of tobacco a Bristol packet had carried to her agent in London last spring. An urge to wear those gowns came over her, an urge that she welcomed with bright eyes as she reached out to catch and squeeze Emerson's hand.

"It will be a vacation, Edmund! A fortnight away from accounts and bills of lading. I'll go directly I've finished and begin my packing."

"Winnsboro shall know of your coming, dearest one. I'll send a rider at full gallop to hire a suite of rooms at the King's Head. You'll be a queen, and I your willing slave!"

Laura Lee nibbled with dainty teeth at the quill pen she lifted. "Billy Joe should see me. Then he'd realize what a fool he was to give me up for a revolt that can't help but fail!"

"He'll not see you, Laury. He's living in a tent somewhere north of the Catawba. What would he be doing in Winnsboro?"

Chapter Four

THE CARRIAGE jounced and rattled along the hard dirt road to Winnsboro. The rolled leather curtains and the cushioning softness of the upholstery lent a sense of intimacy to Billy Joe Stafford and Mistress Deborah Treat. Their belongings—a few silk and dimity gowns for Debby pilfered from Tory plantations and fitted to her figure by a tailoress from Charlotte Town, and an extra suit of uncut velvet, a waistcoat of corded silk, and silver-buckled shoes for him—were in the traveling chest atop the coach.

In riding habit of green silk, with frills of Chantilly lace at throat and wrists, Debby was as regal as any plantation lady. Her perfume was delicate and her muslin cap modishly pleated and beribboned. Stafford still felt the bemusement into which his first sight of her had thrown him, as she swept into the front parlor of the little shingled house that General Morgan had requisitioned. The blonde hair that had fallen in loose plaits to her back was coiled and puffed into a soft golden halo. There was lip rouge on her full red mouth and blue shadow on her eyelids.

The sight of her standing so prim before him, yet seeming so mischievous, with her blue eyes bright and dancing as she felt his admiration, made him remember the days of his youth in southern Virginia. More than once he had gone calling on the pretty daughter of a neighbor, to take her to a dancing assembly. More than once he had stood tongue-tied as he stood then, bowing slightly.

In those days, he had been awkward in modish waistcoat and long frock coat, with his feet encased in silk stockings and buckled shoes. He had been more used to the Indian hunting shirt, in which he slipped through the woods with a Kentucky rifle in a hand, or in open shirt and homespun breeches, crouched on a tall stool before an account bench, working at figures. The care of the plantation was his first chore, and hunting in the woods his first love. Such time as he had for the social amenities was given grudgingly out of the night hours, when he could have been trailing a 'coon with a hound and a lantern.

Stafford wondered at himself. He was no mere youth now, but a grown man, married—he made a grimace—and the sometime owner of a rich plantation. Yet as he stared at Mistress Deborah, his tongue was wooden and his heart a pumping trip hammer.

In that silent bewilderment, he led her to the coach and took his place beside her. Cynically he asked himself if he were a schoolboy again, falling moccasins over poll in love with some tavernkeeper's daughter or ferryman's niece. He had known girls before he had met and wedded with Laura Lee, but no girl had ever touched something deep inside him as this one did.

He glowered at the opposite wall of the coach, glooming on the past, until Debby glanced slyly sideways at him and inquired the cause of his fear.

"Fear?" he replied blankly. "I'm not afraid."

"You sit so quiet, I thought you to be summoning up your courage for our task ahead." She smiled sweetly.

He snorted. "If you must know, it's you. You put a fever in a man. A fever I don't relish."

Idly she picked at a frill of sleeve lace. "You're thinking of your wife, aren't you? She hurt you very badly, didn't she?"

Again he snorted. "No wife of mine any longer! I'm finished with her, as I'm finished with all women."

Debby laughed and leaned her head back onto the upholstery pads. "You haven't even begun with me. I'm your doxy, remember?"

"A crude joke, Deborah."

Her eyes opened wide. "I'm not joking. You told me yourself you'd make me your own personal camp follower."

The coach swung to the thrust of a rut on a wheel, and they came together, so that he had to reach out and hold her to prevent her slipping from the seat. His lips were lost in the fragrance of the yellow hair that came loose from her muslin cap.

"If only you were," he whispered, and then he let her go.

Mistress Treat was discovering that what she had begun with the intent to tease was becoming a runaway horse. She liked this big man with the face that could be infinitely sad one moment and brightly grinning the next. Under her breath she swore at his wife, knowing her words to be unladylike and secretly relishing her naughtiness. If only that slut had behaved herself, she'd not be here in a carriage, riding southward with a man whose touch on her body put a ferment in her blood. She shuddered, remembering her capture by the British soldiers. If his wife had not acted the harlot, then he would not have rescued her. If he had not rescued her . . . She shook her head angrily.

Vexed with her dreamings, she snapped, "When we're done with our business at Winnsboro, I'll relieve you of your promise."

"Ah, and will you now?"

His hand was at the back of her neck, his fingers lost in the soft golden curls, and he was turning her head, and then his mouth was over hers and his lips burned and glowed and she shook in a strange sort of delight that was a mixture of fear and hunger. Like a vise his hand held her while his lips drank from her mouth. Then he whispered, and each word was a fiery brand thrust into her heart.

"Deborah Treat, you're a shameless darling and a great lady and a naughty tease, and if I were free I'd get down on my knees and ask you to marry me. But since I can't, you'll live up to your promise and I to mine."

Dreamily she whispered, resting her warm cheek against his and staring blindly at the flapping coach curtain, "If only it were possible! Remember I'm your sister, brother mine. We're William and Deborah Pickens, fleeing from Francis Marion, who burned our plantation beyond Cross Creek."

He let her go at that, and watched the slim fingers in their net gloves as they set her disarranged skirt to proper fullness. As she bent, her long lashes veiled the sultry hunger in her eyes, and the agitation of the full bosom that pressed into her modesty bit showed that she fought, even as he did himself, to control this moment between them.

Stafford settled his back to the coach cushions and brooded.

The coach was moving now through a countryside of rolling hills covered thickly with towering pines. Here and there a little clearing offered itself, with an occasional log cabin from whose massive chimney black smoke came

pouring. Once they saw a man and woman working together at a stump that was partly out of the ground. Then
the pine-belt uplands were yielding to swamp bottomland,
and the coach wheels whirled between towering oaks, with
pond cypress and pond pine thrusting their branches
through smothering Spanish moss. They splashed across a
fording whose waters ran black from the tannic acid of the
cypress roots, and up onto a rutted road that would carry
them through hills of red clay.

Occasionally they came to a wide, barren swath in the
forest, mute testimony to the awful force of the great hurricanes that sometimes swept up from the Florida Keys,
veering inward from the Carolina coast to expend their
energies on the land. Tree trunks lay uprooted and red
soil lay bare, as though a giant hand had made a playful
swipe at the earth, denuding it of its shielding vegetation.

They made fifty miles that first day, stopping at a ferry
tavern in the early dusk of evening, to dine on hop-in-John
and peach leather. With twenty miles yet remaining of
their journey, they sought their separate rooms and the
big tent beds waiting for them.

For hours Stafford sat by the window of his little bedchamber, staring out at the pine forests to the north, silvered
by moonlight. His mind was restless, giving him no peace.
It whispered that he was married to Laura Lee, though she
had as good as freed him of that bondage by her conduct
with Colonel Emerson. It told him that this golden witch
who traveled with him was fuel to the unrest and the
hunger in him.

He no longer owed a duty to Laura Lee. She had set him
free some nights ago. On stockinged feet he could tiptoe
down the hall and scratch at the door plankings of Debby's
room for admission, as far as his wife was concerned.

Yet something held him back.

He brooded by the window, aware that the contradiction
in him shook him as a wind shakes the ripening wheat,
once this way and then that way. So deep was his con-
centration on his personal problems that he gave no
thought to the spying task that Dan Morgan had set him,
and the information he must bring back to Charlotte if the
rebel army gathering there was to have a chance to save

itself from the experienced veterans Lord Cornwallis would hurl against it.

Toward dawn he threw himself on the soft mattress and fell into a dreamless slumber.

Winnsboro lay in the Carolina upcountry, in a region of long-leaf pines and oaks. Settled little more than a score of years before, it was becoming the center of trade for the frontier settlements beyond the Saluda River. Vast meadows surrounded the town, their grasses rippling in the chill November wind that came along the Charlotte road with the coach that swayed and bounced so easily on its leather thorough braces.

Slaves were working in the field that stretched out behind the great crossroads ordinary with its six massive brick chimneys and mansard roof, where twenty dormer windows protruded like curious eyes from its shingles. They were erecting long plank tables, preparing dirt roasting beds, and stretching lines of rope from which to hang candle trees between the oaks.

"Judging from the preparations, there'll be an officers' ball tonight," Stafford told Debby as they leaned forward and stared at the busy slaves. "They'll be feasting and drinking, and something seems to tell me they won't pay us too much heed." He added, "Which may be a good thing, considering the fact that if we're caught they'll stretch our necks in hemp collars."

Then the coach horn was blowing and the wheels spun on the carriage drive, and slaves were running to take the horses. As the brakes squealed, Stafford forced a grin at Debby.

"Are you ready, sister?"

With her heart pounding furiously, Debby touched the tip of her moist tongue to suddenly dry lips. She nodded, swallowed twice, and whispered, "I've never played the spy before. But I'm ready, Billy Joe."

Her courage made him reach out and tighten his fingers on her hand. Then the door was opening and he came out into the sunlight, turning to extend a hand to Debby, then swinging about to survey a little group of Tory gentlemen on the veranda and four British officers striding across the lawn toward the house.

It was too easy. Stafford found that he was conscious of

a letdown and a resultant increase in confidence as they found an aide and told him the story they had rehearsed all the way from Charlotte. The aide was wearily attentive, as if to indicate that their tale was not unusual. With Stafford he politely cursed Francis Marion, the swamp fox, whose men had burned down his manor house.

However, when he discovered that Deborah Pickens was a sister and not a wife, he became effusive in his pleasure at their visit and abusive toward every rebel from the Dismal Swamp to the Newfoundland fisheries. Eyes bright and cheeks flushed, he insisted that Mistress Pickens attend the ball that evening. He informed them also that while the crossroads inn was filled to capacity, the King's Head tavern was almost its equal for spaciousness and catered to the gentry. However, his offer to accompany her was met with a cold stare from Stafford.

Debby swept off in triumph, a little smile on her lips. Between her fingers nestled an invitation to the officers' ball that evening.

"He seemed most anxious for me to make my appearance, Billy Joe Pickens," she said sweetly. "And if I'm to play the lady spy, please be more circumspect with your haughty looks. You'll frighten away the game."

"I only seek gentility in my sister," he growled. "I'll stand for no simpering flirtations."

He felt her arm slip into his. "Only because I'm your sister, brother dear?" she teased, head tilted sideways.

Stafford was aware of the growing jealousy that ate at him. The slightest admiring glance that a man cast at the chattering Debby as she paced beside him sent a hot rage through his body. He told himself it might have had something to do with the fact that he posed as her relation. Other men could look at her slim ankles beneath the modest petticoats and at the supple waist that swayed so easily to her stride, but he must act the slightly bored brother.

At the King's Head, he discovered that his new relationship was to have its advantages. When he chose their rooms, paying two shillings and sixpence for "house room" and logs to be burned in their bedchamber hearths, he discovered that it was only natural to kiss her as she paused outside her door. He took advantage of the shadows and kissed her soft mouth, rather than the cheek she extended.

"We're to be at the crossroads ordinary by eight," she told him, eyes glowing as she looked up into his face. "It's best not to be late, and so draw attention."

"We'd draw attention if we went early," he said. "I'll knock on your door a little beyond the hour."

In his own room, he removed coat and waistcoat, stretched out on the bed, and was soon asleep. When he woke it was dark. His shout brought a slave with candles, and another slave with hot water and soap and a razor. Seated in a stiff-backed chair, he let himself be shaved and his wig newly powdered.

From his traveling chest he drew out a suit of fashionable mauve velvet and a waistcoat of corded silk with silver buttons. In taut white stockings and silver-buckled shoes, he discovered that he gave every appearance of the gentleman dandy. His white Ramillie wig with its attendant side curls above the temples added the final fillip.

His Harland watch showed a few minutes past eight. Debby would be ready now, in the white satin gown with lace falbalas and edged with modish silver gimp over which she had exclaimed so fervently when General Morgan had shown it to her. Closing the door of his room, he paced down the hall to knock lightly with his knuckles.

"Debby? Are you ready? It's past eight."

Her words came muffled through the door. Taking them for an invitation to enter, he turned the knob and was in the little bedroom before she had time to protest. Debby stood in frilly pantalets that clung tightly to the turn of her hips and fell in ruffles of lace about her thighs. Tight silk stockings encased her legs, with black ribbon garters indenting her flesh.

"Oh!"

She turned, offering him a nude white back and the roundness of her hips pressing tautly into the pantalets. The vision of her full young breasts remained with him as he breathed faster and took two steps toward her.

"Debby," he whispered.

She looked at him over a bared shoulder, seemingly unaware that she was standing directly before the mirror of her dressing table. "I did say I'd be your doxy, Colonel, but I never thought you'd treat me like one."

He fought the hunger in him as his eyes ran from her high-heeled slippers up the stockinged legs to the taut undergarments. Then, as if that hunger were a flood bursting the banks of his control, he came across the room to her and put his hands on her arms, running his palms gently from her shoulders to her elbows.

She stood braced against him, her head fallen back against his chest, breathing more swiftly. A flood of tenderness and wild hunger swirled up from deep inside Stafford, shaking him. He wanted to be gentle and soothing, fierce and wild and savage, all at the same time.

"All Winnsboro looks on me as your sister, Billy Joe!"

"You teased me all the way from Charlotte!"

"The way you wanted me to tease you. You almost begged for it, with your sheep's eyes and hangdog look."

His hands turned her and brought her in against him. A finger beneath her chin lifted her flushed face and brought her mouth so close that he had only to bend to kiss her. Mistress Treat held his kiss hungrily, her moist lips cradling his starving mouth.

Then she was burying her face on his chest, murmuring, "Leave me to my dressing, Billy Joe, or we'll never arrive at the officers' ball."

He wanted to damn the ball, and the job of spying they must do this night. The spool bed was waiting, its blue dimity coverlet neat and crisp, ready for a hand to disarrange. Its mattress would be soft and receptive, its sheets cool to the touch of their fevered bodies. With Laura Lee, he had known the cloying of pure sensuality, but never this fire of need, this consuming thirst to make a girl his own.

Stafford fought himself, and let her go, moving to the window and staring out into the night along the road that wound between the old oak trees all the way to Camden. He breathed deeply, feeling the tightness of his cravat about his throat and the confinement of his waistcoat.

"Dress yourself, then!" he cried hoarsely. "Make yourself as lovely as you can, to tempt those damned turncoats and lobsterbacks!"

His face was flushed with anger and frustration and bewilderment. From the corner of his eye he saw his reflection in the crude glass of the inn window. A Betty lamp, hung on chains from an overhead beam, made the windowpane almost like a mirror. He could see Debby fitting herself into a lacy underbodice and shaking out a

sheer petticoat before slipping it over her head. Muttering
savagely under his breath, he closed his eyes.

When she was done, he turned around. In the soft lamp-
light she was something from the secret yearnings of a
man's youth, when he believed in things like love and
womankind, and the fact that for every man there was one
woman made only for him. The curls of her yellow hair
caught and held the light, making it glitter in each delicate
strand. Her ripe mouth was a dark-red bow above a
dimpled chin and a stretch of soft, creamy throat. The hoop
gown left her smooth shoulders exposed, and clung with
gentle firmness to her slim middle.

Debby curtsied, eyes lowered, aware that his hands were
clenched into big fists at his sides as he fought the temptation to take her into his arms. She rose and pirouetted,
making her belled skirt sway outward lazily.

"You'll be proud of your sister tonight, Billy Joe," she
promised.

The candles that were hung on the cording stretched from
tree limbs in the meadow behind the crossroads inn made
a blazing brilliance of the night. Carriages were scraping
to a halt on the graveled drive, bringing guests in from
nearby plantation houses. Officers were swinging down
from their saddles, indifferent to the fact that no slave
was there to take the rein. Candlelight gleamed on golden
epaulets and on silver buckles, on Medici collars and ribbon scarfs as Stafford brought Debby forward to be introduced, with himself, to Lord Cornwallis.

Charles Cornwallis was a short man, given to flesh. His
scarlet uniform jacket seemed a little too tight, his face
a little too florid. He stood now bowing politely, his smile
affable as he bent before the Tory ladies or shook the out-
stretched hands of the Carolina gentry who had come from
their manor houses to support his attacks on their rebel
countrymen. Popular with his men, easygoing, he was pos-
sessed of a quick mind and good military judgment.

His words to Stafford were soft and agreeable, inquiring
as to his journey, sympathetic at learning that his estate
had been burned out from under him by Marion. He promised vengeance on the swamp fox.

"When we catch him he'll hang! Tarleton and his
Green Horse will do the trick for us. Mistress Pickens, I
hope we do not sound too bloodthirsty to your ears."

Debby let herself languish, employing a little ivory fan over which her smiling eyes flirted at the English general. "La, your worship! I do believe the swamp fox only something conjured out of a bad dream. Who can catch him in those horrid bottomlands where he hides himself?"

The General turned aside and spoke to an aide, who detached himself from the little group and moved toward the big cypress-shingled ordinary. With a smile of apology, Cornwallis swung back to Deborah.

"I've sent for Banastre Tarleton, ma'am. I'll let him tell you himself who will catch and hang Francis Marion. I've no other Light Horse commander fit for the job, but with Tarleton I need no one else."

They remained standing close beside the General until a short, handsome man, whose white breeches and black leather top boots enclosed muscular legs, came walking with a bouncing stride from the inn. Banastre Tarleton was a hated man in the Carolinas. His dispassionate efficiency, which permitted his men to bayonet helpless rebels in cold blood, the manner in which he raged with his Light Horse troops from rebel house to rebel plantation, hanging and burning, shooting and looting, made him a monster to the Americans.

As Cornwallis introduced him, he bowed low before Deborah. Stafford had heard that this Green Horse colonel was a hand with the ladies, and the manner in which his hot black eyes roved about Mistress Deborah made Stafford only too eager to believe the tales he had heard over the campfires.

"Find the fox? Of course I will, my dear. And when I do, I'll hang him high to one of his own swamp cypresses! Come now. Let me find you a bit of hock punch and tell you all about it."

"But—my brother . . ." protested Debby, indicating the glowering Stafford.

Tarleton laughed. "He seems big enough to care for himself." The black eyes left Deborah long enough to assay the rawboned Stafford. There was no depth to those eyes. They were flat and merciless, as the eyes of a snake are merciless. "Eh, my good fellow? There's roast pig out back, and bottles of Canary and Madeira. Flip, too, if you care for the stuff. Now, excuse us."

Stafford watched the green back of the Lieutenant

Colonel move off beside Debby. Fury seethed in Stafford. His eyes did not miss the casual intimacy of Tarleton's hand on her arm, or the way in which he bent above her perfumed hair. As if that were not enough to feed the helpless rage in him, Debby's gay laughter and admiring eyes encouraged and invited his attentions.

"Hussy," he whispered to himself between clenched teeth. "Jade, doxy, strumpet!" He flushed a little at his words, and mentally apologized as he paced around the side of the ordinary to find long plank tables covered with bottles and goblets, and three slaves to serve them to the guests.

He took a bottle of Madeira and a goblet of Wistar glass and went into the ordinary through the wide kitchen door. The entire inn had been emptied of all furniture belowstairs. The taproom was given over to the officers and Tory gentlemen. The adjoining long room, with its deserted bar and polished flooring, was filled with those officers and ladies who chose to tread the minuet and the jigs to the music of a military band.

He mingled with the Tory plantation owners and the British officers, smiling and affable to their nods and stares. He stifled the unhappiness in him and made himself agreeable, engaging a fat tobacco grower in talk of pests and vermin, admitting that the hurricanes, when they came, could ruin a man in half a day, and agreeing that land leased for as little as seven hundred pounds of tobacco was like stealing gold from a man's pocket. A gaunt man in black garments, who was an ironmonger out of Charles Town, regaled him with tales of the profits he was making while molding musket barrels and cannonballs for the English.

Stafford moved through the rooms, bowing sometimes to haughty officers, holding his smile by will power alone at their cold, blank stares. Once he danced with a thin little woman from the Carolina low country, to the strains of a French minuet.

He found himself drinking flip and West India rum, claret and persimmon brandy, in an endeavor to loosen the tongues of the men with whom he drank. But he heard no word of Cornwallis' plans mentioned, or any suggestion that Lord Charley was considering anything for the future other than a partner for the next dance. In disgust, Stafford took a bottle of Madeira from the keeping room and found his way out to the candlelit yard. Idly he sauntered by the roasting pits, shallow trenches dug in the ground and covered with beds of glowing red embers, above which entire sheep and pigs were being slowly turned by grinning little black boys.

Discovering that the fragrance of the roasting meat gave him no appetite, he turned toward a row of benches set in rustic simplicity in a grove of great magnolia trees. Seating himself, he filled his goblet and drained it.

He thought of Laura Lee and Debby and he cursed all women.

"Man can't do anything with 'em, and can't do anything without 'em," he told the wine flask. He regarded the bottle a moment, then poured the red wine into his glass. "I despise a solitary drinker," he told the bottle. "Man who drinks alone has no friends."

He lifted the glass and eyed the rich red wine. Well, Billy Joe Stafford had no friends. Even his personal doxy, sweet little Debby, had deserted him for that monster, Tarleton. Stafford emptied the glass in a frenzy of self-pity.

"Past life's over with," he muttered. "Used to be a comfort to me, fighting under Dan Morgan, knowing Laury was waiting for me at the Hall. No comfort knowing she's there now, with her British lover!"

He was bitter, and in his bitterness he sought refuge in the bottle again. Gloomily he stared at the roasting pits and the plank tables. Everybody here was having a good time. Laughter sounded from the inn, mingled with the strains of a minuet from the long room. He sighed heavily.

"Should be spying out Cornwallis' secrets," he muttered. "That's what I'm here for. Dan wants to know, so he can tell Greene. Don't feel like spying. Feel like drinking!"

His belligerence told him at last that the Madeira was having its effect. He grinned and sipped again at the wine. It was then that he saw a woman in a green taffeta gown mincing toward him. For a moment he hoped she would pass him by, and then the bitterness and the confusion in him changed to cynicism.

He stood and bowed, telling himself that if Laura Lee had betrayed him, and Deborah Treat had abandoned him, he would find solace here.

"You poor, dear man, all by yourself! Are you as lonely as you seem? I'm Mrs. Sevier, from Cheraw." She giggled a little and added, "I'm here all alone, without my husband."

He lifted his goblet and smiled. "I've only one glass. We could make it a loving cup, if you've a mind to share it."

She was perfumed and plump, and anxious to be thought a flirt. Her red lips touched the goblet rim almost with a kiss as he offered it to her, and her dark-brown eyes admired him candidly. She chattered amiably and sat close enough beside him on the bench so that, if he chose, he could slip an arm about her waist.

"I'm late," she informed him breathlessly, "but then, I'm late for nearly everything. My coach drove up just a few minutes ago. More people are coming to the ball than you could imagine. They were still arriving after me. La, I'll wager they'll keep coming until the dawn."

"It seems the Carolinas are sending Lord Cornwallis off in fine fashion."

"Aren't we? Oh, I do hope he and that handsome Colonel Tarleton end this terrible war very soon!" She sighed and stared off into space, and for a moment Stafford saw the worry that lay deep in her eyes. "My son and husband are off fighting with the rebels. I told George before he went, I said, 'I think you're awful, giving up everything we've built, just to be able to say you're a free man.' "

She was another Laura Lee, clutching desperately at the past, and at the advantages that past had given her. For an instant Stafford saw her with clear eyes and knew the fears that bedeviled her lonely nights.

He said, "It seems strange to find a Tory lady with a rebel husband. Couldn't you find an understanding in you for his beliefs?"

It was as though he argued with his wife, trying to understand the emotions that had turned her into a Tory. Mrs. Sevier laughed shrilly and tapped at his chin with her fingertips.

"You'll not engage me in argument, young man. I argued enough with George before he took young James off with him. I told him then, if he wants to give up the manse and the stables and our slaves, our crops and harvests for a dream, let him! Now that he's gone, they all belong to me."

She revealed her greed in the tilt of her dimpled chin. "I'm a wealthy woman. One of the wealthiest in the up-country. When Lord Cornwallis beats the rebels, I'll be even wealthier, with new trade contracts in Charles Town."

"You seem assured of victory, madam." He smiled wryly.

"Anyone knowing Lord Cornwallis and his plans cannot help but own such assurance."

Stafford felt excitement growing in him. Was the fate that had given him cold stares and idle chatter inside the ordinary to be more kindly in this magnolia grove? He inched closer to the woman, who continued to eye him archly.

"You seem to own the General's confidence, Mrs. Sevier," he whispered. "But then, the General, like any other man, is susceptible to beauty."

Mrs. Sevier's laughter was gay. "La, sir! No need for any special confidences with Lord Charley to know what he plans. It's no secret in the Carolinas, among Tory circles."

She broke off and eyed him keenly. "I'm surprised you haven't heard the gossip."

There was enough suspicion in her voice to make him eager to convince her of his innocence. "I've buried myself on the plantation for the past year. Ever since—since my wife died. This is my first venture out of Cross Creek in a twelvemonth. I come only now to give my younger sister a chance to see the world."

Mrs. Sevier seemed reassured. She said, "His Lordship has over fourteen thousand troops under his command. The rebels with Morgan have less than three thousand, even adding in the ragtails General Greene is bringing with him from the North." Her hands spread as she shrugged. "What need for plans, sir? Morgan and Greene will be encamped at Charlotte. Lord Cornwallis will move out of Winnsboro northward. His columns will close in around the town and the rebel camp. The revolution will be over in the South."

"And in the North as well," he commented harshly, "if events mature as you predict."

"You sound unhappy at the prospect."

He recalled himself from his forebodings with an effort. "Not unhappy! Merely uncertain. It sounds too simple."

"It's a simple thing. With officers like that handsome Banastre Tarleton at one column, and Cornwallis himself at the other, how can it fail?"

How can it, indeed? echoed Stafford in his mind. And, as if to help Cornwallis, Nat Greene and Dan Morgan were talking of dividing their small forces!

Mrs. Sevier was laughing intimately. "You poor, gloomy boy! I think you're the one who needed to come out in the world and enjoy its company, not your sister! Smile, now. Take thought on the fact that when the rebels are beaten, you and I will be very rich. Our plantations will be honored with British contracts. Gold will pour into our coffers in a flood!"

Greed and insecurity: these were the forces that twisted this woman, as they twisted Laura Lee. It seemed to Stafford that when a woman married a man, she should be greedy only for him and his welfare. But then, Laury always claimed he was an idealist.

They chattered and sipped the Madeira together, and her bright eyes and loose lips showed that the rich red wine was having its effect on her. Her flirtatiousness became almost maudlin. She rested her head on his shoulder and breathed deeply, letting him discover, if he would, that the white bosom pressing into her fichu was worth more than a casual glance.

Stafford smiled to himself grimly. Aye, they were greedy and clutching, these women like Mrs. Sevier and Laura Lee, but they were also riddled with vanity, which made them act the temptress to whatever man was at hand. He wondered if it had been vanity that had put Laura Lee into bed with Colonel Emerson.

Mrs. Sevier wanted to be kissed. Her face was turned upward, and her heavy mouth pouted prettily.

He said conversationally, "Have you been introduced to Lord Cornwallis?"

"La, no. Nor to that handsome Colonel Tarleton, though I wish I had been. He's dancing attendance on a blonde beauty. A pretty thing, but vapid." She intimated that she was not so scatterbrained. Her laughter was soft. "They were almost kissing when I passed them in the shadows of the stair well. I suppose she's his doxy."

Stafford was rigid in the rage that made his face flush.
Aye! Debby would be playing up to Tarleton, acting the
lady spy and enjoying it. Kissing him in order to loosen
his lips so that they might spill their secrets into her ears.
Dan Morgan had chosen a good spy in Deborah Treat.

And a poor spy in himself, he thought wryly.

Mrs. Sevier writhed closer, fitting her soft thigh to his.
With a forefinger she soothed the line of his chin, then
lightly traced his lips.

"Where are you staying in Winnsboro?"

"At the King's Head ordinary."

Her fingernails were tickling his throat. When she spoke,
it was with a deep huskiness. "I have no room in town. It
was foolish of me to come so unprepared."

She was asking him to bed her for the night, Stafford
knew, but his thoughts were all on Debby and her possible
attentions to Banastre Tarleton. He fought to suppress
the desire to push this simpering thing from him, but he
dared make no scene that would draw attention to himself.

He smiled down at her and said, "Come stay with me, if
it pleases you. I'll have to see my sister first, and warn
her that I'm having a guest." He added with conspiratorial
mirth, "I'll tell her you're an old college friend from William and Mary."

Her laughter let him know that she appreciated his wit,
even as her increased breathing told him that she antici-
pated the night that lay ahead. Her warm fingers squeezed
his hand.

"Hurry back. I'll be waiting."

Stafford rose to his feet and bowed, touching the back
of her hand with his lips. He felt a stab of sympathy for
the woman and for the need that made her throw herself
so recklessly into a stranger's care.

Then he was moving easily between the cooking beds
and past the long plank tables toward the ordinary door.
As he came in the kitchen doorway he paused in stunned
shock.

Entering the front door of the inn, bright with laughter
and in a tightly bodiced green silk gown, her fleshy shoulders smooth as cream satin, was Laura Lee. At her elbow,
waving to a group of fellow officers, was Colonel Edmund
Emerson.

Chapter Five

THEY DID NOT see him. English colonels and captains came surging forward to surround them, bowing and making a leg to Laura Lee, striving to be first to caress the fingers she extended for their lips. Hands caught at Emerson, clapping him with rum-induced joviality. In a moment they were being swept into the long room.

Stafford slid into the shadows, hearing the thudding of his heart in his rib case. Beads of perspiration stood out on his forehead. That had been a near call. He had stood at one end of the tavern hall and his wife at the other. One glance of her eyes and he would have been overpowered and haled before Lord Cornwallis as a spy.

He closed his eyes. His concern was not for himself. He had accepted these risks when he accepted the task General Morgan set him. It was Debby that was his worry. They would take her, too, as food for their hemp ropes.

With a need for haste and silence that made him go pale, he went searching through the ordinary. He must find her before Laura Lee or that British popinjay, Emerson, came sauntering through the halls in search of old acquaintances.

He found Debby and Banastre Tarleton without difficulty. They were whispering and laughing, and seemingly oblivious of the fact that the shadows of the stair well did not hide them from prying eyes. The sight of them added to the ferment in Stafford. His hand balled into a fist, a fist that he would have enjoyed swinging at Tarleton's hard jaw.

No commotion, Billy Joe! he told himself. You're in bad enough straits as it is, with Mrs. Sevier waiting out back for you, and Laura Lee and her lobsterback colonel in the long room.

If Stafford could not use his fist, he could use his foot. He stumbled calculatedly in the dim light, and planted his heel down hard on the polished toe of Tarleton's top boot. The English colonel swung about with an oath quivering on his lips.

"Pardon, Colonel! Excuse me, Debby dear. A headache

coming on. One of my bad ones. Please come along and nurse me."

Tarleton looked down his nose and sneered. "Apparently your brother is less a man than I first thought, Mistress Pickens. Pooh, a headache!"

Debby sighed and looked concerned. "He does get bad ones, dear Colonel. Mother used to care for them. Now it's my responsibility."

Tarleton muttered under his breath and shifted his shoulders.

"Be understanding, Banastre! A cold cloth to his forehead, a little massage at the temples, and he will sleep. Then I'll be back."

He brightened at that promise. "I'll wait impatiently," he assured her, bowing.

Then they were moving between colonels and captains, hearing but not listening to their voices and their laughter. Debby whispered, "Is anything wrong? You came in such a hurry, and with such a terrible look on your face!"

He told her of the arrival of Laura Lee and Colonel Edmund Emerson. "If they see me, our jig is done."

"We'll contrive, then, to become invisible."

They apologized a path to the kitchen door. Hand on her fingers, Stafford drew her past the big hearth to a little door that opened out onto the side yard.

"We'll pack and run," he told her, remembering Mrs. Sevier.

"Not yet," she protested, trotting to stay even with his long strides as he hurried away from the candle-brightened night. "I've other business in Winnsboro, Billy Joe."

Surprised, he swung around, coming to a stop.

"Other business? You mean learning what Cornwallis plans to do against Greene? Ease your mind, my dear. I've already discovered that."

She smiled a little at his confidence. "Not that, no. Colonel Tarleton has been bombarding my ears all evening with the part he's to play in those plans. Do you remember my locket? The locket with the glory hand?"

He remembered the locket, and remembered also that Deborah Treat was down from Philadelphia on a mission of her own. There was something here in Winnsboro securing her interest, something important enough for General Washington to request her co-operation.

Her hand shook him into stride again. As they walked, she whispered, "There's a little house a mile outside town, on the road to Camden. Once it belonged to my uncle, before the British hanged him. I must visit the cellar of that house, Billy Joe."

At the King's Head ordinary they discovered their driver sodden with flip, and so it was Stafford that backed the horses into the traces and buckled the breast straps. With Debby inside the coach, he reined the horses around and sent them trotting through the darkness.

The house loomed up black against the surrounding fields. Twin chimneys thrust upward at either end of the ruins. All that was left of a man and his hopes and dreams, thought Stafford, swinging from the seat to stare at the charred remains of a door hanging crazily on a solitary hinge. Tarleton or another like him did this.

As he handed Debby down from the coach her eyes were wide, misted with tears. Her chin trembled slightly.

"I used t-to come here and play when I w-was a little girl. I can remember the way my uncle laughed when he a-and father got together, and the smell of Aunt Ruby's pies. . . ."

Stafford muttered savagely and pulled her in to his chest, letting her bury her face against his frilled jabot. Between sobs, she whispered, "Over there by the east chimney was a s-swing. My uncle made it for us. On w-winter nights we'd make crackers. Jimmy and Eddie would whittle out the cracker stamps and I'd fit the handles to them. Father loved it here. Said that if he didn't live in Virginia he'd move next door to Uncle Matthew."

He soothed her, letting her talk, knowing it would ease the heartbreak inside her. With her talk she brought back memories of his own youth. Silently he wished that he could have known Deborah Treat in those days. If he had, some of the nightmare through which he walked these days might never have existed.

At last she drew away a little and dried her eyes with a lace kerchief. As she wiped tears from one eye, she looked up at him with the other, and her mouth smiled faintly.

"You think I'm a big booby, don't you, Billy Joe? Crying like this at the sight of a house burned to its foundation stones four years ago."

"You made me remember many things, Debby. Things

about myself I'd forgotten in the business of being a man. What were you like when you used to come here? As a little girl, I mean?"

She forgot her tears as her eyes widened in surprise. Then, strangely, she flushed from neck to brow and her eyelids lowered. Silently she reached out and caught his hand and tightened her fingers on it. Like that, she drew him after her, silently, toward the burned ruins.

"What I want is in the cellar," she told him, "behind a loose stone in back of a broken dower chest."

"You must have been freckled and bucktoothed as a little girl," he said glumly, "if you won't even talk about it."

Serenely indifferent to his words, Debby picked her way over rotted beams and charred planks that fell apart at a touch. Beneath the debris were the stone steps leading downward to the cellar. "It can't be too far from this spot. As I recall, the old dower chest stood just about there. . . ."

He went before her down the stairs, thrusting aside a fallen timber, lifting the remnants of a shattered cider jug and tossing it from him. His hand guided her steps, until they stood on the hard-packed dirt of the old cellar. Now Stafford fumbled with tinderbox and a punched tin lantern he carried at his belt. Kneeling, he opened the tiny metal door, pinched the wick, then applied the flame he had coaxed from the rag tinder to the candlewood match.

The open door of the punched lantern gave off a soft yellow glow that revealed an utter desolation of shattered furniture and torn matting, broken farm tools and wrecked framework.

Debby cried out sharply, pointing.

"The dower chest! It's been moved, and the stone—"

Stafford saw the lopsided chest wedged behind a wooden flax wheel. To one side of it, a stone lay on the floor; a gray stone, roughly square. Above the stone, a gaping darkness yawned.

He knelt and put a hand into the emptiness where the stone had once been embedded, fingers feeling the stones on either side and above and below, and the dirt behind. Debby came and stood near him, not breathing.

"It's gone, isn't it?"

"There's nothing in here, if that's what you mean. What was I supposed to find?"

"Oh! I forgot. Billy Joe, it's only that I've sworn secrecy —not to tell anyone. Just not anyone at all. Otherwise—"

Her dismay and regret showed in the wide eyes that searched his face, and in the lips that trembled a little.

"I understand." He smiled to reassure her.

"It's gone, though," she said, "and all the secrecy in the world isn't going to help get it back. It was a map, Billy Joe. A map my father drew and hid here in Uncle Matthew's cellar for safekeeping. Now please don't ask me any more. General Washington said I wasn't to trust anybody. Not anybody!"

She was like a little girl right now, Stafford thought, as he came off his knees to tower above her; a little girl playing grownup, with her fur-trimmed Nithsdale hood and cloak. Her face was shadowed in the lantern light, her eyes luminous, asking for understanding.

"Now I know what you were like when you were a little girl," he whispered, smiling gently. "You were just as you are now, only much smaller, and perhaps not quite so lovely. Innocent and sweet, trusting and sort of radiant. I wish very much that I had known you then, Deborah Treat. I wish it with all my heart."

Stafford took her in his arms and kissed her soft mouth tenderly. In this moment he realized that nothing else on all the American continent mattered to him half so much as this soft body his arms were straining to him, and the tear-wet lips that quivered so happily against his own.

"Billy Joe! Oh, Billy Joe!"

"Debby, dearest Debby!"

She drew back a little and a glory shone in the eyes with which she searched his gaze, moving them from side to side, smiling and sobbing, trying to reassure herself that what was happening between them was not some taunting dream. Then she flung herself against him, her cheek pressed to his chest, clutching him with her strong young arms.

"Hold me, Billy Joe. Just hold me tight for a little while."

He held her strained against him so that she might draw strength from his big body, whispering to her, pushing back the hood of her cloak so that his lips could lose themselves in the sweet fragrance of her yellow curls. He never afterward remembered what he told her there in the cellar that night, with the punched tin lantern at their feet, but he would always remember the manner in which she lifted her face at last and looked at him, then raised herself on tiptoes to kiss the corner of his mouth.

"Now take me back to the ordinary, Billy Joe. We've a long ride ahead of us tomorrow."

They lost a little of the magic that had been in them as they went up the cellar stair into the night. Realization came to Stafford that if the map was gone—a map important enough to concern General Washington himself —an irremediable blow might have been struck against the American cause. Silently he cursed the seal that Washington had set on Debby's lips. If he didn't know what they were after, or where the map was to lead, how could he help?

The further thought came to him that if the British had found the map, and were going to use it as the Americans planned to use it, any chance for him to help Deborah Treat was gone forever. He did not want to think on the fact that if the map would help the Americans against the British, it would help the British equally against his own people.

Their ride back to the King's Head ordinary was made in utter silence.

Ezra Whipple eyed the empty leather jack that had held the flip now warming his belly. He sighed heavily and let his little eyes roam across the officers and ladies pacing between the plank tables behind the crossroads inn. His second drink was already settling in his innards, and the night was still young. He chuckled, congratulating himself on the forethought that had tempted him to desert the American lines at Monmouth and lose himself here in the Southland, where no man knew his past.

Aye, he'd done the right thing. Why starve and freeze when by changing his sights a man might have as much flip as he'd a mind to drink, and as much roast pork and fowl as he could hold? Taking thought on the fact that it had been a long ride down from the Dan River country with Colonel Emerson and that bold piece, Mrs. Stafford, Ezra Whipple found himself a wooden trencher and carried it to the serving tables. The Colonel and his lady were on the front lawn now, greeting friends. In a moment they would be making their way inside the house for the dancing.

He was turning away with his platter filled high with thick meat slicings when he saw Billy Joe Stafford. In his amazement he almost dropped his meal.

"God's passion!" he swore. "It can't be!"

Whipple was a big, gross man, but there was a stealth to his stride that had been bred in his bones, in the years of his boyhood near the Fly Market in New York, when his deft fingers and nimble legs had made him a master pinchpurse at an early age. He slid now into the shadows and moved around behind Stafford and Mrs. Sevier, his absorption in the food on his platter only half pretense.

Stafford was standing, bowing, smiling. Then he was swinging on a heel and moving away, straight for the rear door of the ordinary. Ezra Whipple waited until his fine mauve velvet coat was gone out of sight before he sidled closer to the humming Mrs. Sevier.

"Beg yer pardon, ma'am. Could you tell me the name of the man yer was talkin' with?"

Mrs. Sevier looked haughty. "It's none of your concern, that I can see."

"Forgive me, ma'am. It's just I thought I worked once for 'im and would like to nod to him for old times' sake."

Mrs. Sevier softened, despite the fact that the gross hairiness and fleshy face of this man caused a slight nausea. "It's Pickens, if you must know. Billy Joe Pickens, from the Cross Creek country."

Ezra Whipple straightened and grinned. "Ah, no. That wouldn't be the man. Though he do look uncommon like the man I knew."

He turned and followed the path that Stafford had taken to the rear door. There he halted, knowing he would not be allowed inside, and gave words to a uniformed slave. The slave went away and came back shortly with Colonel Edmund Emerson at his elbow.

The Colonel was in a pet. "See here, Whipple. Can't have you bothering me at every turn, you know."

Whipple leaned closer and whispered. Colonel Emerson's eyebrows arched and his monocle fell as his mouth opened and closed soundlessly. When the man was done, the

Colonel whirled and brought a hand down like a vise on Whipple's wrist.

"If you're lying, love me Satan, I'll—"

Whipple was ingratiating. "Now, why should I lie, yer worship? Didn't I speak truth once before, when I brought you Stafford's uniform that showed him one of Morgan's men? I hate his black guts even more'n you do. You just want him dead so's you can bed that piece inside legal-like, and inherit his— Easy now, Colonel!"

They faced each other, the Colonel with head flung back and Whipple uneasy. Whipple spread his hands placatingly. "Meanin' no offense, sir. It's just he beat me something awful. No man ever before beat me before at anything. It gnaws inside me, like a mouse in a grain sack. I got to have satisfaction."

"Hmmm, yes. Ah, indeed. Let me think." The Colonel brooded, then turned and stared across the tables at the bench where Mrs. Sevier had been sitting. The bench was empty.

Colonel Emerson said, "It seems one of our birds has flown. Come along. Perhaps the goose will lead us to the gander."

Chapter Six

WHERE THE King's Head tavern fronted the road, a
dozen towering sycamores made a park of the grassy level
that edged its graveled drive. A stone well stood amid the
trees, with its slant roof neatly shingled and its copper-
banded dipper carved in the guise of a human head.
Ezra Whipple and Colonel Emerson waited now in its
shadow, staring at the darkened upper windows of the
inn.

"Damme, what keeps him?" growled the Colonel. "The
woman entered the place half an hour ago."

"Mebbe he waited for her inside," suggested Whipple.
"They seemed uncommon friendly on that bench."

Colonel Emerson shook his head slightly. "It may be, it
may be, but I'll need more proof of his identity than your
eyesight before I'll go barging in there, demanding to
arrest him."

"My eyes are hawk's eyes," growled Whipple sullenly.
"More than one suckling pig and powder horn I've carted
off with me as prizes from musket matches on village greens.
It was Stafford, all right, damn his soul!"

"If he went in, he'll come out, sooner or later," phi-
losophized the Colonel. "We'll wait a bit longer, then make
discreet inquiry." He broke off suddenly to swing about
and stare up the road toward Camden. "Hssst! I hear
coach wheels."

"Aye. Hear 'em myself. Better go round out of the
way, lest we give away the game."

They moved off together toward the springhouse, a sod-
covered structure in which were housed preserves and
gallon tins of milk. Since the sod house lay a little westward
of the ordinary, with a good view of the drive and the road,
they crouched down there, waiting.

The coach screeched to a stop, and the man on the
driver's seat came down and into the glow of the coach's
candle lamps. Colonel Emerson cursed softly under his
breath.

"Stafford! It's Stafford, without a doubt! But in God's
name, what's he doing here?"

71

Ezra Whipple chuckled. "And with as nice a piece of female goods as ever I had the pleasure of laying hands on. Seems like he's taken her over for his own pleasure, after near crippling me for trying to do the same thing."

The Colonel hissed and Whipple ceased his sullen growls. Tense, they watched until Stafford had led Deborah through the wide, white doorway with its classic cornice overhead. A slave stumbled sleepily from the open door and made for the standing horses.

When the coach and four had gone around the corner to the stables behind the inn, Colonel Emerson straightened to his full height and brought the silver-mounted pistol from its holster at his side. He checked its priming, then replaced it.

"Come along, Whipple. We're going to catch ourselves a spy, and see him hanged, come sunup!"

Stafford led Debby up the wide staircase with an aiding arm about her waist. Twice she stumbled in her fatigue and disappointment. On the drive back from the burned house, she had sat with hands folded tightly before her, staring blindly at emptiness, trying to remember.

"The map was in the cellar wall," she told Stafford for the dozenth time. "I know it, I know it! I saw Father put it there, directly after I'd helped him sketch it out."

"The British found it. Before they burned the house, they would have ransacked it."

Her smile was pathetic. "Then all my trouble's for nothing."

They paused outside his door, and she let him take her into his arms and hold her. "Not for nothing, perhaps," she whispered gently. "At least, I've found you."

The latch lifted under his hand and the door to his bedroom opened. As the door swung wide, the light from a Betty lamp came out into the hall with them, and showed a woman sitting in the big tent bed.

"Mrs. Sevier!" said Stafford harshly. "I forgot about her and her promise to share my sleeping quarters!"

The woman in the bed was clad in a sheer night robe, through which the flesh tints of her body were visible. At sight of the girl with Stafford she cried out, and drew up the sheets and quilted comforter from her lap.

Debby was stiff with shock. She brought her eyes from

the woman to Stafford, and now the softness and the tenderness was gone. She hissed, "Is a bedding down what you promised her in exchange for the gossip she gave your ears about Cornwallis?" She would have thrust herself from him except that his hand was strong on her arm above the elbow, turning her and forcing her into the room with him.

Stafford closed the door, then swung on Mrs. Sevier.

"Madam, I compliment your industry," he said, "while regretting its misdirection. At another time, you would have found me dancing with impatience."

He wanted no shouting, screaming woman to summon attention to his presence. The dark glances Mrs. Sevier was casting at Debby, who stood white-faced and rigid at his elbow, were warning signals he could not disregard. And so Stafford stepped forward to the edge of the wide bed and knelt. He reached out and caught her soft white hand.

"My sister is young and something shocked at worldly manners in her brother," he said softly. "You'll forgive her concern because of her youth."

"She seems no sister to me," sniffed Mrs. Sevier. "Not the way she looks at you with those big blue eyes, and the hate she has for me!"

"Debby, tell Mrs. Sevier you're my sister."

He spoke without turning his head, hoping that Mistress Deborah Treat were enough the actress to catch his cue, and act upon it. He sighed with relief when he heard her speak.

"My brother is correct, ma'am. I am his sister. I beg you to forgive my impulsive emotions. You see," and her voice broke in a sob, "Billy Joe is all the family I have. Father and M-mother d-died and there wasn't anyone to t-take care of me, excepting B-Billy Joe."

Stafford swore softly through his teeth. Actress? She was as accomplished as any woman who ever trod the boards with the American Company at Charles Town!

He saw the suspicion in Mrs. Sevier fade into compassion, then melt to pity. Now when the woman looked at him, he read coldness in her eyes.

Debby was weeping softly into her kerchief. "He always takes me with him, then abandons me as soon as he sees a p-pretty face. Three times I've had to f-find my way home from distant places. Once even from Charles Town! He stays away weeks at a time and always comes home drunk. Sometimes he—he hits me when he gets l-like that."

Deborah Treat sobbed and Stafford groaned inwardly, telling himself that now she was overdoing it. Mrs. Sevier swept back the bedclothes.

"Shut your eyes, you scalawag!" she hissed, and stood up. She went to Debby and brought her in against her shoulder. "You poor dear! No need to tell *me* what men are. I know all about them!"

Stafford stared from where he knelt at the bed, assuring himself that this was surely a nightmare in which he moved, for even as Debby opened one eye to glare furiously at him, the door behind her was opening and Colonel Edmund Emerson was standing framed in its trim. A pistol was fitted in the fingers of his right hand, and the barrel of the pistol was aimed very steadily at Stafford.

Billy Joe Stafford closed his eyes, then opened them. The fleshy face with the black hair and little pig eyes that he had seen last in the long room of the Black Thistle ordinary, some miles above the Dan, was gloating at him over the Colonel's shoulder.

"I'm asleep and dreaming," he told the room.

Debby and Mrs. Sevier caught the dismay in his voice and whirled. Debby's hand came up to her lips, muffling her sharp outcry, but Mrs. Sevier was under no such compulsion for silence. She screamed.

Colonel Emerson let his eyes laze over her body in its thin nightrail. "Scream again, my dear. Rouse up the house. It's what I seek most to accomplish."

Mrs. Sevier paused and stared. Moistening her dry lips, she asked, "Who are you? What do you want?"

Emerson bowed. "A colonel in the Thirty-third Foot, madam. Here to arrest two rebel spies. Colonel Billy Joe Stafford, of Morgan's Rifles, who makes a practice of traveling out of uniform, and the little camp follower he appears to have attached to himself."

"Aye, that she is," broke in Whipple at his shoulder. "Her that was too good for me, the blonde slut!"

Mrs. Sevier crossed the room and snatched up a quilted robe, engulfing herself in its folds. Her hands trembled as she fumbled, tying its belt. "He told me he was a Tory gentleman. A plantation owner from Cross Creek, burned out by Francis Marion. One of Morgan's men? I can hardly believe it."

It was then that Debby slid to the floor in a boneless crumpling.

Stafford moved as though her fainting were a signal. The little iron Betty lamp, shaped like a Greek bowl with a snubbed, curving spout and filled with explosive camphine, was in his fingers. The next moment it was being hurled at the door with all the force of his powerful arm. The camphine went up in a burst of brightness a little more than halfway across the room.

Its noise was deafening. The sudden blackness that descended erupted with Mrs. Sevier's shrieks and the Colonel's harsh curses. Stafford was across the room, kneeling beside Debby, when her hand caught his wrist and stayed him.

"It was only an act, Billy Joe! I saw you looking at the Betty lamp and wondering whether your hand could beat his pistol."

"Then come after me, as fast as you can!"

He dived for the doorway, hunched low. He struck Colonel Emerson in the bow of his ribs, his right fist traveling six inches and thudding deep. The air went out of the Englishman and then Stafford was thrusting him aside and stepping on his leg as he fell, moving for Whipple.

The Colonel was only half blinded by the lamp blast. He had been in the hall, where the light of a few tallows in their iron wall sconces helped to shield his vision. As Stafford rammed into Emerson, Ezra Whipple backed up three steps and freed his long knife from its sheath.

Whipple came to meet Stafford with his knife blade naked, a wolfish grin disclosing his stained teeth. He feinted and swayed, putting his weight on the ball of his left foot. Like that he left his feet, dropping to his knees and stabbing upward for the unprotected belly of the plantation owner.

"I'll open your gizzard, Stafford," he howled in his triumph. "Then I'll take your doxy for myself a week or two, until I tire of her. After that—"

He grunted as a spasmodic lunge took Stafford clear of his point. His blade slashed empty air. He landed heavily and turned, on one knee, to discover Stafford unbalanced and falling, hitting the stair rails with his back.

Whipple was after him like a hungry cat, seeming almost to spring from his knee for his prey.

Stafford saw him coming; saw and rolled forward hard, using the stair railing as a springboard. The knife came down at him, but now he was on his back and his hands were moving up and wrapping long fingers around Whipple's wrist.

As Whipple panted, crouched over him, trying with strutted muscles to dig his steel into the unprotected throat below him, Stafford tried to roll again. He found himself pinioned by the deserter's thickly muscled legs.

Whipple grinned at his helplessness and put his bulky shoulders behind the knife. He rasped, "After I'm done wi' her flesh, I'll let the British have her neck to put a rope around. Mebbe I'll be doin' her a favor, at that. When I'm finished with her, she'll be glad to hang!"

Stafford found purchase on the hall plankings with his feet. Slowly he arched his back, carrying the bigger man with him. Panic showed in Whipple's face. He tried to bear down more heavily, to force that living bridge flat against the floor; tried and failed, and, in trying, lost the grip of his own feet.

Whipple went flying, back to the stair rail.

Stafford hit him like that, standing before him, in that moment of paralysis when the rail caught and held him. He hit him five times, three clubbing rights to his belly and two short, chopping hooks to his jaw. When he stepped away from the deserter, Whipple's limp body sagged to the floor.

Debby was at the curve of the stairs where they ran down to the lower hall. Doors were opening. Sleepy faces were poking out at them. Voices cried out, asking questions, pleading for quiet.

"Billy Joe! Hurry!"

He needed no encouragement. He was at her side, racing down the stairs after the slim ankles her lifted skirts and petticoats freed for speed. They skidded about the knobbed newel post and made for the rear door that opened toward the stables.

"Pray our coach horses haven't been unharnessed," he told her.

The slave whose task it was to groom and water the horses of the guests had been awakened from a sound slumber by Stafford. Half asleep, his fingers became thumbs as he worked, so that when Stafford and Debby came flying out of the night at him, he had done little more than unfasten the headstalls and loosen the trace links.

Stafford brushed the man aside, his fingers racing over trace buckles and harness straps. Then he was stepping to the driver's seat and lifting the whip, chirping to the horses. Their driver would be safe enough, Stafford knew. No man could identify him, and by morning he would slip away to rejoin them at Charlotte .

The coach lurched into high speed as the horses dug dirt with their hoofs. Behind them, Colonel Emerson would be recovering, roaring for a detail of Light Horse to go after them. Those cavalrymen would traverse the roads eastward to Camden and north to the Waxhaws.

Stafford swung the coach to the south, toward Savannah and the Georgia settlements.

Chapter Seven

THE SUN came up over Thicketty Mountain to touch the long rifles of the Maryland regulars and Virginia militia where they lay at breakfast some miles from the Broad River, at Cowpens. They had come fast during the night, luring Banastre Tarleton and his green-jacketed cavalrymen as a bait lures the fish. They lay now, relaxed and easy, watching General Dan Morgan and Colonel Billy Joe Stafford walk among them.

Morgan was in a sweat of fear. Always before a battle he grew afraid. It had been this way at Quebec and again at Cape Diamond, where he had knelt and prayed in the snow. His eyes looked longingly at the forests that flanked his troops. Nervously he licked his lips.

"I'm for taking a walk, Colonel. Over to the woods yonder. Make the last check of the boys by yourself."

Stafford nodded, his thoughts turned inward. As he strolled among the buckskinned Marylanders, his eyes automatically studying their shot pouches and powder horns, he was remembering that wild ride from Winnsboro, still hearing the creaking rattle of the coach wheels carrying them southward.

He and Debby had circled about below Ninety Six, and freed the horses. Abandoning the coach, they mounted and rode along the banks of the Saluda, skirting Fort Prince George to cut east by north. Riding day and night, they had reached Charlotte in two days.

Debby had been exhausted. He had carried her, half asleep in his arms, into the house from which she had emerged as his sister. Haggard himself, with his beard stubble uncut, he had sought out Morgan and General Nathaniel Greene, to tell them the result of their journey.

Greene had been exultant, pacing the tent, his scabbard clanking at his heels. "We can do it, Dan! Split up what forces we have. You take the Marylanders and the Virginians. Find Tarleton. Run ahead of him until he comes after you. Play the fox to his hounds. Let them find your campfires still warm. Leave a few odds and ends behind, as if your men were terrified."

They had broken camp after that, with Greene taking his troops to Hick's Creek, seventy miles east and north of Winnsboro. Morgan and his riflemen marched west, to the juncture of the Broad and Pacolet Rivers, through a region of pine woods and rolling grassy slopes, inter-woven with bubbling mountain streams.

Stafford went with Morgan, to scout ahead of the slim column.

They flushed Tarleton out of Winnsboro by sending in spies with word of where they were. As Morgan had an-ticipated, Cornwallis was beside himself with delight at the news. Banastre Tarleton and his Light Horse would finish off Morgan, while he himself would attend to Greene.

For almost a week they had run before the English cavalry. Now it was time to draw the trap shut. Colonel William Washington, whose dragoons had acted as skir-mishers to harass the little bands of Tories that roamed the hills and so keep Tarleton's rage at fever pitch, came clattering through the camp, waving an arm at Billy Joe.

"The lobsterbacks are coming up the road now," he shouted. "Neat and pretty as if they were on parade. Dan says to wait until they come at us. Their red coats will make better targets once they're out of the woods."

Stafford waved an arm and the Marylanders and Vir-ginians came off their backs and rumps to trot toward the slopes, where they would make their stand. They were rested and fresh, full of confidence. All during the war, these men had faced no troops that shot as well as they, and none whose courage was greater than their own. Their breakfasts were warm under their belts, and most of them were grinning and shouting cheerful insults at each other.

Morgan ordered the Marylanders and the Virginians to the top of the hill. The Carolinians were to be stationed below, behind a hasty bulwark of logs and branches. They had come in during the night, most of them, with Colonel Andrew Pickens. These men were full of hate for Tarleton, for they had scores to settle with the green-coated riders who raped and pillaged and looted their homes and the homes of their neighbors. Out ahead of both lines were McDowell and Cunningham, commanding expert mountain marksmen.

Stafford found Dan Morgan emerging from the woods,

where he had been praying. He went with him down the line of troops as Morgan spoke to them in a firm voice. "Shoot straight. Two rounds each ought to win us the victory, so be steady."

The men hooted at him and laughed and Morgan grinned at Stafford. "The devil could bring his fellows out of Hades, Billy Joe, and these boys would send them running back."

The sun was growing warm overhead at this midmorning hour. Here and there in the forest below, the waiting riflemen could see the flash of sunlight on polished cannon barrels as two big grasshoppers were wheeled into position. Now the laughter and the chattering slowly hushed. Men rubbed their thumbs along the lengths of their rifle barrels to deaden any reflection of the sunlight in their eyes as they squinted over the sights. Some men brought out leaden balls from their shot pouches and put them in their mouths, to prevent thirst. They squirmed and twisted in the grass, lowering themselves to give the British as little to shoot at as they could.

A cannon belched, and a wisp of white smoke plumed upward from the woods. Another cannon joined it, and soon the dull thudding of the artillery formed a background to the sudden shrill shouts of the English soldiery that came bursting through the forest underbrush in straight lines. Bayonets glinted from their muskets.

McDowell roared an echo to the shout that Cunningham made. The riflemen at their sides squeezed triggers and a wave of flame and lead hit the front rank of British infantry. Men went down in little clumps, ripping gaping holes in the lines. Now the Americans were firing as they willed, as they had learned to shoot in these same hills that they now defended, firing at cautious deer or even more elusive wood ducks. Those scarlet coats of the Seventy-first Foot and the Seventh Regiment were a lot easier to see than the bobbing white tail of a Virginia deer or the rainbow coloring of a marsh bird.

"By God, they can take it," grunted a lanky mountaineer, pausing to shake powder from his horn into the muzzle of his rifle.

The man beside him held his breath as he squeezed his trigger, then crouched down to growl, "Then let's give it to them."

They came up together, rifles poking through the branches of a felled pine. The rifles spat their flame, then sank back out of sight.

Now these men were moving back, folding in behind the Carolinians under Pickens, who thrust their own rifles forward to take over the brunt of the fire. They broke the charge that Tarleton hurled at them, driving the British regulars into panicky confusion. Tarleton had no choice now but to commit his reserve under McArthur to the fight.

The deadly rifle fire of the Americans was an awful thing to the English. It seemed that every small round iron barrel that came thrusting at them over a fallen log or between the branches of a felled tree seemed to know by instinct where to aim. Men dropped with hot lead in their chests and bellies, or buried inside their skulls. Fingers clawed frantically at bloody dirt as men gasped out the last moments of their agony. Officers went down, leaving the long lines of charging men leaderless. Bayonets were useless against such concentrated fire. The regulars hesitated, confused.

McArthur brought his reserves up to flank the Virginia militia that held the crown of the hill to the right of the Maryland rifles. Colonel Howard collapsed his men back toward the cavalry under Colonel William Washington, until Tarleton and McArthur committed themselves by a charge. Then Howard whirled and his men knelt and their rifles came up.

That one volley crushed the British reserves. As more than half their comrades fell away from them, the others whirled and fled. Now it was the turn of the Americans to fix bayonets and follow, and their faces lit up. These men who ran from them had delighted in pillaging their homes, in raping their wives and sisters, in burning food and stores it had taken a lifetime to collect. Bayonets clicked into place. With an exultant roar, they raced downhill after the redcoats.

Banastre Tarleton heard that tremendous shout just as he was bringing his cavalry down on Colonel McCall's Georgia mounted militia. Deep inside him, he sensed that it was the American victory cry. To add to his discomfiture, he found himself face to face with the dragoons commanded by Colonel Washington. Sabers clashed as horses reared and men fell backward out of their saddles with shoulders and faces hacked bloody with cold steel.

During the battle, Billy Joe Stafford had been stationed with the Virginia rifles. Now, as they swept past him after the fleeing British regulars, he whirled and let his eyes hunt for a riderless horse. Colonel Edmund Emerson might be somewhere down in that melee below. He wanted very much to see Colonel Emerson right now, when the lust to kill was strong in his blood, and a man could kill another and blame it on the battle.

He found a big dappled gray gelding with its saddle empty and swung up, reining the horse around and kicking it with a moccasined heel. The gray went down the slope at a breakneck pace, and Stafford craned his neck to study the tall black leather caps of the running soldiers. Only the Seventh and the Seventy-first were with Tarleton here at Cowpens. The Thirty-third Foot, of which Emerson was a colonel was with Cornwallis at Turkey Creek. Stafford did not know this, but when he began to suspect it, he reined the gray up along the edges of the Mill Gap road.

It was here, while his eyes vainly searched the last of the fleeing soldiers, that three green-coated dragoons from Tarleton's command came down at him from the woods. He recognized the stocky man who rode between the other riders, his saber like a whip of light as he waved it.

"There's one of the bloody rebels!" Tarleton yelled.

Then they were on him and Tarleton's saber came slashing down, but Stafford used his rifle barrel to deflect it, touching the trigger of the rifle when he saw a face framed around the barrel.

Tarleton recognized him for the rebel spy he had been in Winnsboro even as the dragoon at his right stirrup fell away with his face blown off. Hate and fury contorted his features and he swung his saber twice, back and forth, in blinding slashes. Then a pistol ball whistled past and Tarleton shouted, "It's those damned farmers and clerks under Colonel Washington!"

Tarleton and his single companion spurred down the road as a dozen Continental dragoons went clattering after them.

When Stafford recognized Colonel Washington, he stood up in the stirrups and shouted, "It's Tarleton himself,

Bill! Go get the monster!" He relaxed, letting the small of his back settle against the saddle cantle. At mention of that name, he could see men stiffen in eagerness. Banastre Tarleton was the one prize every man jack in the army wanted.

Stafford shook himself. He was an officer in the army that was chasing Tarleton and what was left of his regulars back to Hamilton's Ford. It was his duty to be with his men, not moping here by the side of a dusty road, waiting to find the man who slept with his wife.

He turned the gray and went after the Americans. He was in time to see Colonel Washington exchange saber thrusts with Banastre Tarleton, and see Tarleton ride away with his hand all bloody. Then he was in among his own men, reloading his long rifle from the saddle, kicking his legs free of the stirrups and dropping down to run from fallen log to standing tree, firing at the scarlet coats that made such good targets to his woodsman's eyes.

They followed the British until dusk came creeping like a gray fog among the pines and evergreen laurels, putting a shimmery haze on the woods, coating the glossy leaves of the shrubs with silvery dust, hiding the rotting humus floor of the forest. Men appeared suddenly in that mist, and just as suddenly faded again, making further pursuit impossible.

Stafford came back slowly through the woods. Night was darkening around him, and a cold wind was sweeping across Thicketty Mountain. Here and there, red fires were being built, and men were bringing out tin cups and spoons and hunting knives against the hunger in them, as stew began to simmer in the great iron cooking pots.

Colonel Washington was stretched out on the ground, his back propped against a tree while a man worked over a pistol wound in his knee. Dan Morgan stood above him, looking down at the torn flesh. He swung around as Stafford came up, his broad face alight with triumph.

"We cut them to ribbons, Billy Joe! Took their cannon and twenty-five officers and hundreds of regulars prisoners. Ha! They talk about Burgoyne's defeat up North. Wait'll they hear of this!"

"The Tories will go into hiding quick enough," Stafford agreed, crouching down to watch a bandage being wrapped about Washington's knee.

"Tarleton did it, damn his eyes!" explained the Colonel, wincing a little. "Turned and fired a pistol at me after I slashed his sword hand. But he'll carry my mark until he dies!"

They were not aware of it as they gathered around the fires, these men who sipped gratefully from tin cups of steaming coffee or dipped bread crusts into bubbling stew and speared floating bits of meat with sharp hunting knives, but Cowpens was to rank as the turning point of the fight for the South. Cornwallis had lost his left wing at King's Mountain. Banastre Tarleton had cost him his right, here at Cowpens. The Tories who wavered between outright allegiance to the crown and a diffident tolerance of the rebels would go into hiding.

Dan Morgan sipped reflectively at his tin cup, his pugilist's face split with a grin. "Now maybe Nat Greene and I can do something about Debby Treat and her mission down here. We've given Lord Charley enough to keep him busy, regrouping his men and making different plans. The pressure's off until the next fight, and that's the best time to spare a good man."

Stafford lifted his head and stared. "This mission must be almighty important for it to be such a secret. I don't even know myself what she's after, and she won't tell me."

Morgan stood and put a hand to Stafford's shoulder. "Come for a walk with me, Billy Joe. I've things to say for your ears alone."

Stafford rose to his feet and trailed Morgan's bulk between the red fires. Men lay stretched on their backs, staring at the dark sky and moving branches overhead, or groaning against the wounds staining their bandages red. Some slept exhausted, while others huddled around the fires, reaching out for more coffee and stew. There was an air of informality about the camp that made Stafford contrast British discipline with their own.

He spoke of this to Morgan's back as his eyes roved the encampment. "Their officers would never walk like this among their men and let them sleep or eat or do whatever else took their fancy. Yet these farmers and shopkeepers put those regular troops to rout today."

"Aye," agreed the General heavily, stepping over a prostrate man. "We've little discipline and even less al-

legiance. A man can pack up his gear and go home when
the mood suits him, and be reasonably sure nobody will
come after him, to hang him for desertion. We don't even
have regular uniforms, though I've heard it rumored that
General Washington is drawing up plans for them. But it
isn't the uniform that makes the soldier so much as it is
the man inside it."

Now the camp was behind and the dark forest close
before them. Stafford lifted a branch and held it to one
side as Morgan ducked through onto a narrow footpath.
He said, "They do only one thing well, Dan. They shoot
straight."

"Maybe that's the thing the British keep forgetting.
Parade tactics and bright uniforms and polished boots
look good to the eyes, but when the time comes that men
stand face to face with the lust to kill in them—why,
then give me the men that shoot true to the target!"

They came out of the path to the bank of a little lake,
where the water was as still as the surface of a mirror.
Along the bank, towering pine trees stood like lonely sen-
tinels. A fish plopped in the gathering darkness, stirring
ripples. In the distance, on the far side of the lake, the
forest stretched as far as the eye could see.

Morgan put a foot on a fallen log and touched a hand
to the pocket of his blue uniform jacket, feeling for the
Bible that he habitually carried. "If we had the money
and the good food the English have, we'd have won this
war a long time ago. Or maybe we wouldn't. Sometimes
a man fights better when his belly touches his backbone
and he's worried about his next meal, or whether his wife
and children have been killed and his home burned. I
don't know. All I do know is that our army down here
in the South is poorer than the proverbial church mouse."

"You didn't bring me through the woods to tell me
that," Stafford said dryly. "Or maybe you keep forgetting that I served with you from Quebec to Cowpens.
I've some faint memories of starving side by elbow with
you on that march up into Canada, and chewing milk-
weed sprouts and boiled cattail seeds because I was so
hungry I couldn't see straight. I remember Valley Forge,
too, and the time I shot a rabbit and cooked it and passed
the meat and the stew around to my men because I felt
they needed it more than I did. I know we're poor."

Morgan sighed and seated himself on the fallen log. Running his heavy hands along his tight buff breeches, he squinted upward at the moon. "Ought to be a full moon in a few days." He grinned. "Maybe I ought to let Mistress Treat tell you herself what I'm going to tell you, Billy Joe, but if there is a full moon, you won't want to be talking about swamps and dead men with her."

Excitement built a pulse beat in Stafford's throat. He could feel the blood pumping in his veins as his eagerness mounted. Now at last he was to learn what Debby sought here in the Southland. That map they had failed to find in her uncle's cellar wall—perhaps now he would discover what was on it.

"Swamps and dead men," he said softly, squatting down to sit on his heels with his legs bent under him. "Tell me about them."

"The story begins about ten years ago, on the Treat plantation. Alexander Treat was a cantankerous old ruffian—I saw and heard enough of him during our march with Braddock on Fort Duquesne to last me a lifetime—but he was a patriot. He saw war coming. Maybe you've heard him speak out in town meetings about the Townshend Acts and in support of the Sons of Liberty movement? Well, then, you know the old fire-eater."

Alexander Treat hated the English for what they were doing to their colonies. Again and again, he liked to proclaim that George III was treating them like slaves, like a conquered people rather than as his own subjects. In his rides through the countryside, or when he went north to Boston and New York on business, or to the ironworks around Baltimore and to the shops in busy Philadelphia, he took the temper of the men and women around him. Soon, now, men like Sam Adams and the members of the Sons of Liberty in Boston would strike back at the King, who tried to foist mildewed tea from the warehouses of the East India Company down American throats, who sought to push an army of occupation into the staid homes of Boston citizens ("His own countrymen, mind you!" Alexander Treat was wont to scream, with his wrinkled face all scarlet with helpless fury) after his soldiers had shot down their neighbors during the massacre in front of the customhouse.

In his own Southland, the farmers were fighting Governor Tryon. In Philadelphia and Newport, Alexander Treat knew many of the men engaged in smuggling Dutch tea into the colonies so that its citizens would not have to pay the tax on the British product. Oh, there were signs all over the place for a man who wanted to see them. And Alexander Treat, whether he wanted to or not, was peculiarly fitted with the type of vision that was not blind to the future.

One day Alexander Treat saddled a sleek young mare and kissed Mistress Debby—she would only be a child of about fourteen then, thought Stafford, dreaming a little of her ripe red mouth and bright blue eyes—and went riding off down the little lanes and bypaths of Virginia and the Carolinas. He stopped a while in this house and in that plantation, in corner stores and town mansions, and when he came out he carried bulging sacks of coins. Massachusetts shillings and Maryland sixpences, Carolina halfpennies and the big Spanish coins they called Portygee Joes: all found a haven in his brown saddlebags. He took golden guineas and golden sovereigns, silver pieces of eight and copper farthings. Nothing was too much or too little for Alexander Treat, for he was not taking the money for himself, but for the people of his country.

Morgan drew a deep breath and sat brooding at the tree stumps at the edge of the lake. "I guess you could call him a great man in his way, Billy Joe. Most men who make a lot of noise don't mean a word of it, not deep down. He did. He went to a lot of trouble to get that money. Money that was earmarked for us."

It began to make sense to Stafford. Now he remembered what Debby had whispered to him in the ruined cellar of the old house in Winnsboro. "It's a map, Billy Joe. A map my father drew and hid here . . ." she had told him.

"The map shows where Alexander Treat hid all that money," Stafford said suddenly, hitting his knee with a clenched fist.

Morgan turned to stare at him. "Oh, you know about the map, do you?"

"I know we hunted for a map and that it wasn't where we went to look for it. Maybe the English took it when they burned the house down."

"If they did, they're plaguey quiet about the fact,"

growled Morgan. "Had they found it, they would have let us know soon enough, to discourage us. No, I think the money's still where Treat put it, and that the English, if they did find the map, don't know what it refers to. Maybe the thing went up in the fire. And if that's the case, we can forget about the gunpowder and shot we need to buy, and the food and equipment for the men, and the woolen blankets and the new shoes and everything else."

Stafford stood up and let his gaze move across the lake to the little splash where a hunting osprey broke the surface of the placid waters. Exultation blossomed in him.

"No," he said softly. "No, I don't think we need forget about those things. Because we don't need a map to find that money, Dan. We don't need a map at all!"

Chapter Eight

Dᴇʙᴏʀᴀʜ Tʀᴇᴀᴛ stretched lazily in the big poster bed with its flowered valences and matching coverlet. The sunlight streaming in through the curtained windows was putting a laziness in her blood that made her yawn and burrow a little deeper into the sheets and big crazy quilts that sheathed her nightgowned body. Mmmm! That had been a dreadful dream last night, that one about herself and Billy Joe, dancing together without any clothes while the British officers had taken potshots at them with their service pistols.

Her cheeks flamed red as she remembered the manner in which Billy Joe had kissed her as he had gone off with Dan Morgan and his Virginia rifles to find Banastre Tarleton. If only he were here now, to find her so warm and fragrant in the bed sheets!

"Heavens, Deborah Treat!" she whispered. "You scandalize me!"

Her laughter rang out, and then she was throwing the comforters off and sliding her slim white legs out into the cool winter morning. For a moment she stood shivering, debating whether to risk the cold January air by stripping off her linen nightrail by the bed, or keep it on to dress under it.

The goose flesh on her arms won out, and with a giggle she ran for the dressing alcove. In a moment the nightgown went flying through the air and the frilled pantaloons were being pulled up over her rounded hips. She wondered at the hour, knowing it was early, for the sun had not yet touched the headboard of her bed, as it did every clear morning close to eight o'clock.

As she opened her door, the fragrance of sizzling pork patties made her quicken her pace. She ran along the hall floor, carpeted with painted canvas, and down the narrow stairs, past the framed samplers hanging in neat rows on the wall.

Mrs. Wilkins, the widow with whom she roomed here in Charlotte, would be waiting in the big kitchen at the back of the first floor, bent before the big hearth and stir-

89

ring a mess of hominy grits in the big iron kettle on its hanging crane, or turning the spit that held the roasting pig. She would have almost a dozen berry pies baking a golden brown on the hearthstones by this time of day, and crisp loaves of bread covered with a cloth on the kneading table.

There was a man with her in the kitchen, a big man wearing a pale buckskin hunting shirt that was the uniform of the Maryland and Virginia rifles. Her feet paused and her eyes flew to the long rifle standing on its butt plates near the court cupboard and the powder horn and shot pouch lying beside it on the shelf.

Then the man was turning and Debby leaped forward, her eyes and face lighting up. Her arms flew open and Billy Joe Stafford was catching and lifting her up with his hands spread under her armpits. She felt his mouth warm and hungry on her own and she let herself sink into the kiss slowly, carefully, not caring whether Mrs. Eliza Wilkins was shocked or not.

When she could, she pulled her head back, feeling helpless and liking it, being held a good foot off the floor.

"Billy Joe. Oh, please. Dearest—let me go!"

Mrs. Wilkins was making noises in her throat as she bent with her back to them, thrusting a poker at the glowing logs in the fireplace.

"For a hungry man, such as you told me you were not less than two minutes ago, you scalawag," she said, "you can squeeze the life from a woman better than anyone I've ever seen! What would you do on a full middle?"

"She's better than food, Mrs. Wilkins! No roast pig or slice of beef ever did this to me!"

Debby flushed and wriggled and made faces at him, whispering, "Let me down, let me down!" but Stafford only laughed at her.

"Take the broom to him, Eliza!" pleaded Debby.

"Sure, I would if he wasn't so big and handsome," sighed the widow. "But I couldn't bring myself to hurt such a fine figure of a man."

Stafford carried Debby to the thick-planked table and plunked her down in a chair. Mrs. Wilkins was smiling at them, her head tilted to one side, giving gusty sighs as if remembering her own youth. Then she turned and filled two wooden bowls with oatmeal.

"Eat that, the two of you," she told them, "while I slice off a dozen bits of pork bacon and fry you a fine mess of eggs. They tell me lovers can't eat, but the finest lovers I ever knew never paled at the sight of food."

While they ate, Stafford told them of the battle of Cowpens, and how Morgan and his men had broken Tarleton. Now Morgan was moving fast to join forces with Nathaniel Greene, while Lord Charley Cornwallis, believing that Morgan and his sharpshooters were out to capture Ninety Six, was moving in an exactly opposite direction.

"Lord Charley will find out his mistake and turn around and chase Dan. But Dan's too smart to let himself get caught by British regulars. He'll be all right."

Something in his manner made Mistress Deborah regard him sharply. "And why aren't you with him, helping him elude Cornwallis?"

Stafford grinned. "Dan told me the very night of the fight that I'd be a lot more valuable to him buttering up to you. Said it was a patriot's duty to keep the womenfolk happy."

She giggled, then grew serious. "It isn't any such reason! Now out with it."

He bobbed his head at Mrs. Wilkins, and Debby nodded. They ate in silence, except for the extravagant compliments that Stafford gave the widow on her cooking and Debby on her looks. When he could, he caught her hand with his and held it, and his eyes were hungry as they roved across her flushed face.

Then Mrs. Wilkins was shooing them from the kitchen, telling them she couldn't think with all this mooning going on right under her very eyes. In the hallway Stafford swung Debby into his arms and took her mouth with such blind hunger that she went limp and clung to him with fingers that sank their nails into his buckskinned back.

"I've dreamed of this every night since I rode off with Dan for Cowpens," he whispered into her mouth. "Even while I was sighting at a lobsterback, I kept wishing I were with you."

"Coward," she whispered back. "Wanting to hide behind a woman's skirts!"

"It wasn't hiding I was thinking about."

"Why, Billy Joe! How bold you've grown!"

"Soft you are, and warm, and it takes all the will power in me not to pick you up in my arms and carry you to the bed you sleep in!"

They whispered softly, and kissed, and strained against each other, as if they could ease the fever in them by their very closeness. Stafford trailed his kisses from her mouth to her soft throat and up behind an ear until she had to fight to break away, her blue eyes glowing.

"You unnerve me, sirrah! Please, keep your distance!"

To belie her words, Debby flung herself at him, clinging tightly to his shoulders, looking up into his face, whispering, "Ah, Billy Joe! Billy Joe! I don't want to keep you away from me, believe me. I'm most shameless and unmaidenly around you. But we must keep our senses for a little while."

"Then let me tell you why I'm here."

She caught his hand and took him at her side through the hall and parlor to a little recess where bookshelves stretched from the floor to the ceiling. There was a wide bench built into the bookcases, and here she seated him, with her back to the sunlight streaming in through the curtained windows.

"Now tell me." She smiled. "The house is quiet, and Eliza is safe in her kitchen. None's to hear but you and me."

"You know everything I have to say, except one thing. I'm here to help you find those treasure chests."

She cried out, "You know about the money?"

"Dan told me. He had to tell me, Debby. The time's come for us to find those chests."

Her hands caught at the silken kerchief she wore tucked into her bodice and drew it out. As she talked, her fingers twisted and pulled the fine Holland linen into a hundred different shapes.

"We can't! We can't! The map wasn't where I thought it was. How can we find them without a map?"

He hunched forward, his hand moving to capture her nervous fingers. "That's just it. You and I don't need a map, Debby. The British do, but we don't!"

She stared at him as if he had broken out with the pox. "Not need the map? If this a joke, Billy Joe?"

"Remember when we stood in the cellar of your uncle's

house in Winnsboro? You said something then that makes me believe we can. Remember, we were going up the stairs of the King's Head ordinary. You said, 'The map was in the cellar wall. I saw Father put it there, directly after I helped him sketch it out.' Do you remember that?"

"Well," she said hesitantly, her attention caught by his gravity. "I do remember it. A little."

He went on eagerly, "Was it true, what you said? Did you held him sketch out the map?"

"Why, yes. You see, I—"

Debby broke off and sat rigid. Her eyes widened, fastened on his face. Then she was laughing and standing, crying out, "What a big looby-pate I am! Of course! I did sketch it out for him. I drew that map myself. Why can't I draw another? That's what you mean, isn't it?"

She threw herself into his arms and laughed and wept a little, shivering against him. Ever since the night in that ruined cellar, she had been blaming herself for her failure. General Washington had been so grave, so concerned, with his bluish-gray eyes fastened almost hypnotically on her as he insisted on her success. The rebels were poor men. They did not have the financial backing of an empire such as George III ruled, and so they needed whatever money they could put their hands on. He had so bedazzled her that she felt that by failing him she was almost as much a traitor as Benedict Arnold.

Now that Billy Joe was offering her a chance to snatch success out of failure, she grew charged with ecstasy. Her lips rained kisses on his chin and mouth. She panted, "I'll fetch a quill pen and inkhorn. We'll sit down right now and I'll reconstruct that map from memory!"

Her skirt rustled as she swept from his arms to run to the walnut slope-fall desk. She took out a pewter inkhorn and quill pen from the rack that held them.

Stafford swept the crocheted cloth from the round parlor table, clearing a space for Debby to spread her sheets of foolscap, and placed inkhorn and inkstand on two corners, to keep the paper in place. Then she sat, dipping the quill pen into the ink, and began to sketch rapidly.

"The Dismal Swamp is in the northeast corner of the Carolinas, close by the ocean. It's a desolate place. Nobody ever goes there, except a runaway slave to escape a harsh master," she said.

Stafford knew the Dismal Swamp. It was a quagmire of water and marsh grass, hanging Spanish moss and thin green reeds, tall cypress trees and cedars, stretching from Albermarle Sound northward well into Virginia. It covered more than two thousand square miles. Washington himself had surveyed portions of it, back in 1763.

"Father picked it for his hiding place. No Britisher knows these marshes, and few colonists. We went in by way of the Pasquotank River, to a hillock of firm ground, where two big cedars stood."

Her pen point scraped and scratched. Occasionally she paused to stare helplessly at the curtained windows when her memory failed. A fever of haste was in her to set down the contours of the swamp as she had seen and helped draw them. There had been a fallen cypress about a mile into the swamp. They had turned their flat-bottomed scow eastward for about one hundred yards at that point to pass under a low-hanging growth of heavy moss.

"Three big cypress trees stood at one end of the little pond that Father selected for his hiding place. At the opposite end was a stand of black gum trees. In between was a pool of water, with a bit of grassy ground rising in the middle of it. Father moored the boat and stepped onto that patch of land. He didn't have to dig very deep. It was like spooning mud, until he reached a ledge of rock beneath. He said that when the earth was created, the good Lord put that stone there for his especial benefit. He took it as a good omen."

Gradually the black lines and crosses on the foolscap grew into a definite design. When she was done, Debby leaned back and closed her eyes, a faint ache pulsing at her temples. She could hear Stafford bending over the map, murmuring to himself, committing it to memory.

"We'll leave at once," he told her, folding the paper and thrusting it inside his buckskin jacket. "I'll get a horse for you at the livery stable, and ask Mrs. Wilkins to fix us some food."

He broke off to eye her frilled gown with a dubious eye. "Have you clothes you can wear?"

"A pair of men's breeches and a shirt would be the best thing," she murmured, flushing slightly. No woman who valued her modesty would go traipsing about in men's clothing, but this was an emergency. Debby told herself that she would not have Billy Joe leaving her behind on such a venture.

He grinned. "You'll make a fine boy. A little more rounded here and there than is normal, but I'll be satisfied with the result."

Debby stuck her tongue out at him and flounced across the parlor to the hall staircase.

The wasteland stretched ahead of them bleak and barren, with a few scrub pines and lonely elms standing black against the gray sky. Behind them, the rolling countryside of great oaks and long-leaf pines was yielding to a world of green reeds and marsh waters. They had left the last dirt road long ago, and now they galloped across an empty desolation where only the soft pounding of their horses' hoofs broke the eerie silence. Faintly they could hear the lonely cry of a blue heron.

They reined in at the brink of a shallow ford, seeing the water stretching out like a silvered mirror, broken into a hundred little streams. that eddied lazily under hanging mosses and between grassy banks. This was the southwest corner of the Dismal Swamp, which ran for uncounted miles between the Pasquotank River and the sea. Towering cypress trunks and slender maiden cane formed a background of high boles and green foliage, their reflections in the placid waters giving an effect of underwater shrubbery.

Prodding the horses with their toes, they moved through shallow waters that were the color of old wine from the myriad roots and dissolved bark of age-old trees.

"The Yeopim and Pasquotank Indians use dugout canoes to traverse those waterways up ahead," said Stafford, "whenever they have any occasion to go into them. That isn't often, because they think ghosts and dead people haunt the deepest parts."

Debby shivered in her thin lawn blouse and brown coat and breeches and moved closer to Stafford. She seemed a somewhat plump boy, with her rich mane of gold hair tucked up under the battered tricorn Eliza Wilkins had found in her attic. "I was six years younger when I went in here last," she said. "It didn't seem nearly as scary and lonely. Besides, it was summer then."

He put an arm around her and hugged her against him

as their horses splashed through the water. "We should have stopped at one of the grog shops in Elizabeth. A couple of threepenny drinks would have you clawing at the chance to find a spook."

She laughed a little at that, and kissed him impulsively on the cheek. "If I'd as much as a penny's worth, I'd have fallen out of my saddle long ago. Now let's find the dugouts that Daddy hid somewhere around here six years ago."

Debby was a little surprised to discover that the appearance of the swamplands were not as she remembered. A stand of white cedar trees was gone from the hill where they had stood for centuries, and the logs that had clogged this water entrance to the swamp had been swept away. Her eyes ran up and down the moss-hung stream, and she frowned thoughtfully.

"It's different somehow," she said, "but I can't lay a finger on the change. It's so many little things. We hid the dugouts under a little log cairn Daddy built low to the ground and covered with sod, but I don't see anything that looks like it."

"We'll start checking all the mounds."

It was Stafford that found it, by poking a thin sapling branch down in the soft mud. A few thrusts of a spade uncovered some rotting logs. Then it was the work of half an hour to uncover the front of the log shelter that had filled with rotted vegetation. He was sweating when the dugout floated in the water, for the wood, though light, had been half sunk in thick ooze.

They took the spade and a saddlebag filled with food, and the two Indian paddles that had been hidden beneath the boat. Their horses they unsaddled and hobbled. Then with steady thrusts of the paddle Stafford sent the dugout in under the thick drapery of Spanish moss.

The Dismal Swamp was a tangled mass of tall cypress trees and live oaks hung with gray mosses that trailed spidery tendrils in the water. The land quivered like jelly when a man walked on it, and what looked like land was sometimes only marsh grass. Southward, a great expanse of reeds blew forever in the winds off the Atlantic, earning itself the title of the Green Sea. The farther they slid through the smooth water, penetrating deeper into the great marsh jungle, the larger became the trees.

The smell of decay was all around them. No birds flew

here, and no animals hunted between the woodbine thickets. It was a dead and desolate place. Quiet lay like a cloak on the water and the trees and on the dense underbrush.

As he bent his head to avoid the touch of a fallen cedar, Stafford grunted, "Your father couldn't have picked a better hiding place if he'd had the whole world at his fingertips."

"I think he picked too good a place. I'm lost already!"

Stafford searched inside his hunting frock for the map and handed it to her. As his paddle dipped and rose, she bent forward, scanning the lines she had drawn.

"We can't be going wrong," she said at last. "The map's exactly as I remember it. I did see a stretch of fallen trees back a ways that I marked down. Up ahead, there should be a forking of the stream, where we turn right."

The dugout nosed a silent path through pale lavender water hyacinths into a pool bordered by the white skeletons of dead trees and branches. Beyond a mass of swamp moss seeming to grow from the water itself, the pool split into two narrow waterways.

Debby cried out and pointed, and Stafford swung the boat obediently. Now the way was easier, for fewer trees blocked the flowing water, and the sky was open up above, letting in air and a fresh breeze. Stafford sent the boat surging ahead with powerful strokes.

"It isn't far now," Debby called out. "Just beyond the next turn there's a quicksand bog, and beyond it a hummock of firm earth. That's where the chests are buried."

She sat straighter and her eagerness was evident in the little hand that clutched the gunwale of the boat with such strength that the knuckles showed white through the skin. Stafford smiled and sent the dugout skimming through the water.

Thick gray moss, dangling like a rotted blanket from an oak branch, was a curtain that hid the bog from their eyes. Debby put a hand to it, thrust its streamers aside, and cried out in dismay.

In a moment Stafford glided through the hanging moss. He lifted the paddle and sat staring. There was no quicksand bog, no grassy hill thrusting up from the pale sands. As if a giant hand had come thrusting down out of the sky to crush them, hundreds of tall cypresses lay tumbled

in a jungle of dead and broken trees. Their branches made
an impenetrable mass of twisted wood. There was no sign
of any bog, no hint of a little hill.

"It isn't the same place at all!" cried Debby, shrinking
in upon herself in despair. "I was all wrong!" She turned
to him and there were tears in her eyes. "I made a mistake
somehow. B-but I could have sworn I was right. Did we
make a wrong turn? Now we'll have to do it all over again.
And that will take us weeks. Even months, in this crazy
swamp!"

Stafford edged the dugout close to a twisted mass of
fallen trunks and stepped out on them. Carefully he made
his way along the smooth boles between the tangled
branches. When he came to the edge of the great open
space, he let his eyes move across it. Where the trees lay
across the earth he saw jagged white inner wood, where
the bark had broken away. He knew only one thing that
could crush a forest flat like this, and at the thought in his
mind, his excitement flared.

He began to run forward through the tangled jungle of
branches and twigs, lightly, as an insect skims the water,
making his way toward the center of the clearing. Here he
knelt on a tree trunk and scanned the water below.

He broke off a thin bare branch and used it to probe
the waters. In a moment the broken end struck hard
against something.

Stafford stood and waved an arm to Debby.

"You were right, after all!" he roared. "I think the
chests are here below this tree!"

He went to meet her, triumph surging in his veins.

"But how could it be?" she asked, eyes roving his face,
asking for reassurance and afraid of not getting it.

"Hurricane!" he told her with a grin. "Every year they
come up from the Caribbean, veering inland across the
Carolinas. And those big swamp cypresses grow so tall out
here toward the middle of the swamp that they go down
like ninepins when those winds hit them. One good blow
and all your tallest trees went down."

She paused beside him as he took the spade from her,
staring around at the broken wreckage of old cypress giants
with new eyes. Where they lay the thickest, the ground beneath them stood the highest, covered over with a scant
few inches of swamp water.

"Billy Joe, you're right!" she cried out, her eyes feverish with excitement. "A hurricane would do this. Somewhere a natural dam went down and water came flooding in, to cover the mud."

He took her with him across the tangle of sleek gray trunks, her hand held tight in his. Then he was thrusting at the tangled branches, using his long hunting knife to slice and hack until he cleared a four-foot circle in which to swing the spade.

The mud came oozing back as he scooped it out. The dense thickets of tree branches were a help now, for he plastered them with mud. When his spade hit metal, he shouted. He dropped down in the mud, bracing his feet wide, trying to find support in the brown mud.

As his moccasins struck solid footing, he looked up at a scarcely breathing Debby. "I'm on that flat rock your father found. Won't be long now."

His hands dipped deep into the quagmire and found purchase on the big iron handles. Three times he tugged, with the sweat standing out on his face and his muscles straining. Then the chest came loose with a great moist sound and mud dripped from it in thick brown blobs as Stafford swung it high and let it come down hard on the nearest cypress trunk.

Debby was on it with a cry, hands scraping away the mud, bending to shovel handfuls of water over rusted iron bands and thick cypress planking. Then the lock was giving to the key she held, and the top went back.

The chest was filled with coins. Leaning forward, Debby plunged her fingers in them up to her palms, wriggling them, laughing as she heard the faint metallic tinkle that answered her movements.

"There are two more of them, Billy Joe! Two more fortunes under the mud that will win us independence from England!"

"Guns and powder and shot, warm clothing and good food." He grinned tightly. "That's what I see when I look into that chest."

He swung around and his hands went back into the wet mud. This time it was easier. The second chest came up to rest beside the first. In another moment the third chest was beside them, and Stafford leaned against a thick tree branch, breathing heavily.

Debby was plunging her hands to the wrists into the coins now, lifting them and letting them trickle back into the opened chest.

They stood like that, frozen into immobility, when they heard the musket shot. A moment later a voice was shouting at them, "Surrender! Surrender in the name of His Britannic Majesty, George the Third of England!"

Stafford straightened abruptly. A file of red-coated soldiers was moving from flat-bottomed boats across the tangled jungle of fallen cypress trees, rifles at their hips.

Chapter Nine

COLONEL EDMUND EMERSON stared haughtily at the sullen slaves who stood straight and defiant before the seated figure of Laura Lee Stafford. Inside him, a hell of frustration raged. For some weeks, ever since that night at Winnsboro when Billy Joe Stafford had beaten him into insensibility with his fist, the need for vengeance was a red hunger gnawing at his middle. Those weeks he had spent with Lord Charles Cornwallis at Turkey Creek, readying his regiment for service against the rebels, but promising himself that when the time came, he would hunt down Billy Joe Stafford and kill him with his naked hands.

That promise of revenge kept him patient. When a wild-eyed Ban Tarleton had ridden into camp, with word of his defeat at Cowpens, and Cornwallis, in a fury, ordered out his columns, he remembered Stafford. Emerson would ride with those columns, to hunt down and find Nathaniel Greene and Dan Morgan, and smash them utterly. He would also find Stafford among those ragged Continentals, and kill him.

In a sense, then, Colonel Emerson almost welcomed the news of Colonel Tarleton's downfall. It meant less time before he faced Billy Joe Stafford across the field of battle. Contentedly he made his preparations, relishing the high polish his orderly was bringing to his black knee boots with grease and rags, enjoying the sound of his service sword being honed. He even hummed to himself as he strode across the encampment to inspect his command.

And then, on a murky February morning when the world was cold and gray with mist, Lord Cornwallis summoned him to his tent and almost broke his heart.

"I'm relieving you of your command, Colonel," Cornwallis told him, his heavy face dark and savage.

"But, sir—"

"Damme, don't oppose me!" Cornwallis hit the flat of his tent desk with a hand. Worry ate in him. He had come south from New York with high hopes of crushing the Americans in the South, of moving up from the Carolinas through Virginia while Sir Henry Clinton, in command of the army in New York, came down at the head of his seasoned veterans. Somewhere between the Jersey flats and the Virginia hills they would flush out what was left of Washington's rebel army, and the French officers and regulars who served with him, and annihilate them.

Now Ferguson was gone, and the flower of Tarleton's Light Horse dead before these eternally damned rebels who shot as if the devil himself guided their long rifles!

His palm tingled where it had struck the desk. The pain fed his anger, so that he shouted, "Every officer I have tells me what I am to do! I'll not have it, understand? I stand in command until the King relieves me!"

"Yes, milord. Of course, sir. I meant no—"

"Then listen to what I have to say, sir, and oblige me!"

Cornwallis reached among the papers cluttering his desktop, bringing out a folded length of foolscap that he spread wide, placing an inkstand on one end and a silver buckle on the other. His forefinger tapped the map.

"We took this from a house cellar in Winnsboro, back in '76. Hanged the man who owned it, and his family with him, before we could question him. However, from what our Tory friends tell us, the map was drawn by a Virginia planter named Treat. He went among his rebel friends collecting a fortune, intending to use that money against us, if war ever broke out.

"War broke out, but by that time Alexander Treat was dead. This map was left at his brother's house for safekeeping. We hanged the brother."

Colonel Edmund Emerson found himself interested despite his inner anger. He came to stand at Lord Cornwallis' elbow, studying the map.

"The Dismal Swamp," he read. "An ungodly place, sir. I've heard Mrs. Stafford mention it. It lies partly in southeastern Virginia, partly in the northeastern tip of the Carolinas."

The General tapped the paper with a finger. "That's where Treat buried his chests. A damned infernal hiding place, which only a damned rebel would think of!"

Emerson said cautiously, "But if the map was found in '76, why have we waited all this time to concern ourselves about it? Surely we must have made an effort to discover the chests in all that time?"

"We *have* made an effort! Three of them, to be exact.

Each time the dundering idiot in command of the expedition comes back to report there's no such place as the map shows. Each man tells us there's only a mass of fallen trees to be seen. No hill where the chests are hid."

"Yes, sir."

Cornwallis eyed his colonel with a cold eye. "You ask yourself why I pick you out to tell you this? Because circumstance forces me, damme! I've lost Ferguson and the command I gave Tarleton. News of their victory will encourage the rebels. They'll have those mountaineers and their damned rifles swarming out of every farmhouse and hamlet by the dozens. They'll be making efforts to find those chests themselves. I've just learned from Philadelphia —there are a few friends of the crown left there, thank heaven!—that Alexander Treat has a daughter. General Washington sent her south, back in October. Why else but to locate the treasure her father collected for the rebels?"

Cornwallis leaned back against his chair, breathing harshly. "You must find those chests before the girl gets them, Colonel. I choose you because you are somewhat familiar with that section of the land. Your friend Mrs. Stafford may even lend you slaves to guide you. Take a column of the Thirty-third with you, as well as a supply waggon and all needed provender for men and animals. I've nothing else to say, except—bring back that money!"

Now Colonel Emerson stood straight and stiff in the Stafford parlor, staring at the sullen slaves. His fist was clenched on the braided sword hilt at his hip as his lips thinned to a hard line.

"I'd lash their backs to a pulp if they were mine, Laury," he said harshly. "That would teach them obedience."

Laura Lee waved a hand and the glowering Negroes withdrew. "We can't force them, Edmund. The Dismal Swamp is the hiding place for runaway slaves. It's an unwritten law in their world that none of them will ever betray those among them who seek refuge there."

"But how am I to find my way into that place without guides?"

She came to her feet to move back and forth across the thick Savonnerie carpet. Emerson watched her, appreciating the gentle sway of her curving hips that the side panniers of her blue polonaise gown could not conceal, and studying the outward thrust of her bosom in its lingerie fichu with the bright eye of a connoisseur. Ah, well! Once Billy Joe Stafford lay dead, and this infernal war was over and done with, he would be master of these sullen slaves and rolling acres of tobacco land. And master, too, of this proud woman with her smooth flesh showing below the Medici collar, framed in its clasp.

Colonel Emerson made himself affable. "I'll get along, somehow. There'll be Tory friends between here and the swamp, willing to take me through its waterways for a handful of silver."

Laura Lee swung about and stood with her back to a dark mahogany commode. Her brown eyes were avid with curiosity. "You saw Billy Joe in Winnsboro, Edmund. You told me there was a woman with him, if I remember correctly, though we had no chance then to discuss it."

"Two women," chuckled Emerson, eying her carefully. "One in a nightrail thin as the morning mist, the other a blonde slut he picked up outside the Black Thistle tavern, according to Ezra Whipple. He has the blonde woman for his doxy, if I mistake not."

Laura Lee brooded, remembering the quick jealousy that had flamed in her when Emerson had told her first about the girl, back in the Winnsboro tavern. They had been surrounded by officers then, with men cursing and running about, trying to gather enough soldiers to go in pursuit of Billy Joe and the rebel woman. Now they were alone. It was a chance to reveal at last what had festered in her mind these past few weeks.

She came across the room to the Colonel, lifting her hands to place them on his uniform lapels and leaning against him so that he could feel her softness. "You'll not be marching out before morning, Edmund?" she asked softly, letting the invitation glow in her eyes.

The Colonel felt his pulse quicken. He could look down and see her parted lips, the feverish brightness of her brown eyes. His thighs felt her thighs, his chest the heaviness of her breasts. This woman was a walking temptation to a man, with her perfumes and soft flesh and her dark beauty. No man who called himself a man could resist her.

Colonel Emerson whispered, "I'd hoped to hear you say that. I'd been planning to stay over, if you were agreeable."

"I could be even more agreeable, dear Edmund, with the proper co-operation."

There was something in her voice that puzzled him. He frowned a little, trying to concentrate, but he could not think when he held her in his arms like this. As if suspecting his thoughts, she laughed and moved lazily against him.

"Poor Edmund! Am I such a distraction? I'll go hide behind a curtain."

He would not let her go, tightening his arms about her. "Tell me what's on your mind, Laury."

"Murder!"

The word went out into the room and chilled the air.

Her eyes glinted up at him, half in mockery, half in anger. Colonel Edmund Emerson let himself sink into those dark pools, seeking the answer he must have before he spoke.

"Well?" she whispered. "Well? Do you find the thought so distasteful?"

He laughed explosively and brought her against him, bending his mouth to grip her lips. For long moments he held her like that, until they both were shaking. When he loosed the grip of his arms, she lay against him limply, staring upward.

"It's been in my mind since the night he danced with you and I stood in the ballroom doorway with his uniform in my hands," he told her. "I've hunted him across half the Southland. I always catch up to him, but I can't hold him long enough to finish him!"

"No man can," she whispered. "It will need a woman."

His eyes widened. "You?"

She smiled mockingly, her rich red lips curving sensually. "What other woman could fetch him running, Edmund dear? He's angry at me now, for he found you in my bed. But don't you think he's thought about that discovery until he's almost mad? Suppose I were to invite him to visit me?"

"You think he'll come?"

"He will come, and come gladly."

Her laughter was rich and heavy at his gloomy headshake. She went on: "I know just what will fetch him to my side, and when he's here, one of your men will kill him. That Ezra Whipple. He hates Billy Joe, from what you've told me. He would be the one to do it, if he can shoot."

"He's the best man with a rifle in my command. He'll welcome the chance we give him!"

"Then tell your man to be ready when I send you word. I myself will arrange everything. I will have Billy Joe here . for his rifle."

Laura Lee put her soft white arms around his neck and dragged his lips down to hers. She whispered into his mouth, "When Billy Joe is dead, you and I will marry, Edmund. With my money, we shall travel to London and Paris. We may even buy you a baronetcy. Money has been known to accomplish such things."

His palms were roving over her hips as she went on: "I stifle to death of boredom here! I have more gold than I know what to do with. Once this revolution is over, you and I shall learn to live. You'll teach me what London society is like, and what to do when my wealth wins us an introduction to royalty. I can never have those things while Billy Joe is alive. He must die so I can inherit all this property legally, before any court in the land."

For once the Colonel was not thinking of Stafford Hall and its fields of tobacco. He was more concerned with this woman who writhed against him, sobbing softly, demanding that he aid her with her unlacing, that he undo the garters holding up her thin stockings, and driving him into a very frenzy with the sight of full white breasts behind the tissue linen of her modesty bit. Her voice was a whip that drove him to obey, knowing that in his obedience he would find an ecstatic forgetfulness.

Next morning Colonel Edmund Emerson mounted his black gelding before the pillared portico of Stafford Hall with Laura Lee smiling contentedly at him from its wide, shallow steps. There had been no chance to converse further on the murder she planned. Last night she had been a fleshy dervish in her bedroom, making him forget everything but the fact that he played Liber to her Venus.

This morning at breakfast there were slaves all about them, and Colonel Edmund Emerson knew something of the fierce loyalty of the blacks for Billy Joe Stafford. And so the murder they had whispered of yesterday afternoon remained only a remembered word between them.

Still, the Colonel told himself as he cantered down the drive ahead of his troops, he could make certain plans, knowing that Laura Lee had already approved them. He would seek out Ezra Whipple on this expedition to the Dismal Swamp and acquaint him with those plans. He knew the New Yorker would snatch hungrily at the chance to put a ball between Billy Joe's eyes.

Colonel Emerson sat straighter and whistled a few bars of "Maggie Lauder." He had not felt this exuberant in months. Soon now, Billy Joe Stafford would be dead and he would be master of these rolling acres.

The 150-mile journey to the Dismal Swamp became less and less of a task. It began to take on the aspects of a holiday: a week to the swamp, a few days in it to find the chests hidden there, and then a week to get back to the Stafford plantation. The Colonel promised himself the pleasure of adding a few days at the end of that time to rest with Laura Lee from his labors.

They cut south along the Roanoke, then swung due east at Halifax to reach the rim of the great morass. Here Emerson consulted his map and confessed himself at a loss. Now he understood why those other, earlier expeditions to this swampland had failed: The map was inaccurate. Nothing stood where it was shown on the foolscap, even though he flung relays of men working in pairs up and down the swamp searching for landmarks.

Two of his scouts found three hobbled horses and a log dugout that had held a boat. Emerson ordered up the flat-bottomed boats and his men moved into the stream. He intended to learn what these visitors wanted in the bog, the thought occurring that they might be of some service to him. Local residents might know of landmarks that had vanished with the years.

Colonel Emerson could not believe his eyes when his boats emerged out of the forking stream to the mass of fallen trees. A man and a young woman in a tricorn hat, out of which heavy yellow hair was tumbling, and clad in blouse and homespun trousers, stood in the center of that twisted morass of fallen trees and swamp water.

Triumph rose hot and thick in his throat. The three chests, waiting for him to take them! Billy Joe Stafford, alone with that blonde doxy he favored, waiting to be killed! No need for murder now. What he would do would be done in the name of war. He could even be married when he returned from the Dismal Swamp to the Dan.

Hoarsely Colonel Emerson shouted, "Forward, you men! Kill the man! Kill him, understand? And the woman."

A hairy hand caught at his arm. Ezra Whipple peered up from under shaggy brows. "Give her to me, Colonel!"

"Go get her, then." Emerson chuckled, and watched to see the man he hated shot down before his eyes.

Chapter Ten

As STAFFORD saw those red coats moving in the swamp-land, he stood stunned. A dull despair was in him, for his eyes counted close to forty men advancing from the flat-bottomed river boats. Alone, he could not fight them. They would get the chests of gold and silver that the colonists needed so badly. Not only that, but they would shoot him down like a village-green target unless he stirred himself.

His hand at her wrist brought Debby with him on the run. There was no time to pick and choose their path. They bulled through the twisting branches and heavy twigs, stumbling and slipping. Her tricorn came off and her yellow hair made a flow of gold down her back.

The lobsterbacks were shooting now. Their balls whistled overhead and thudded into rotting wood, the whiplike crack of their muskets lifting into the still air of the swamp with dull reverberations.

"This way, Deb!"

He cursed the confidence that had let him leave his own rifle in the dugout. The useless powder horn bobbed at his side, reminding him of his stupidity each time it thumped his ribs. If only he had a weapon to his hands, he would lose a little of his helplessness.

A ball touched his shoulder, cutting the buckskin of his hunting frock. That had been close. Someone back there was shooting straight and true, not just lifting a musket and banging away. Then he remembered Ezra Whipple. He turned in the shelter of a leaning cypress, letting Debby slip past him while his gaze raked the oncoming Britishers. There: in the homespun coat and breeches, his long rifle tilted as he fed the muzzle with black powder from his horn. That was Ezra Whipple.

Stafford cursed as a musket ball sent bark chips and wood splinters into his face. Then he was ducking, using the leaning log as a blind, angling his run for the nearest stream. Once he could get to one of those moss-hung waterways, he would have a chance.

He could not run fast, but neither could the redcoats. He was a woodsman, used to treacherous footing, and his eyes picked out the easiest path with the sureness of a wild animal. He aided Debby in a leap over a tangle of interwoven cypress branches. A man was crying out hoarsely, screaming obscenities back there. That would be Colonel Emerson, thought Stafford, seeing his quarry getting away.

They hit the water in a leap without waiting to plumb its depth, and sank to their waists. It was slower going now. The mud bottom was slick and oozing. A musket ball spanked the water at his elbow. Another hit a hanging twig overhead, and dropped it on his head.

The hanging moss was only a few feet away.

The musket balls were coming closer. One touched Debby at her side, making her cry out sharply. A fire burned in his own where another touched him.

"Just a little more," he gasped hoarsely.

Then the moss was brushing their faces and falling behind like a gray curtain, hiding them. Under its shelter, Stafford drew Debby to the nearer bank.

"We can make better time on shore," he panted, lifting her. "Once we've put some distance between us, we'll take to the streams again, so we'll leave no footprints."

They ran through a small clearing of marsh pinks and ducked under a great white oak whose branches were thickly draped with dangling gray streamers of Spanish moss. Swamp lilies made motes of color here and there, like white teardrops frozen against the glossy green leaves beneath them. The eternal silence of the swamp was all around them. Only their own footfalls made sound.

Stafford drew Debby to him, where he leaned into the thick trunk of a white cedar. Her breath was ragged, almost sobbing.

"You hurt?" he asked after a moment, when he felt the tumultous banging of her heart grow more even.

"My side. A ball touched me there. I—I think it's bleeding."

"Here. Let me have a look."

He made her stretch out on a length of saw grass and unbutton her lawn shirt. A flush sat on her cheeks as she parted it, feeling his eyes moving over the expanse of smooth white flesh she revealed. The musket ball had scratched her side, scraping a wet red furrow across a rib.

"We'll need herb roots and a clean bandage," he told her.

He was like a surgeon in his coldness. It took an effort of will to keep his eyes from the round white breasts pointing up at him and from the curving hips her loosened breeches did not hide, but he was concerned more with her health than with her beauty at the moment.

"Wait here. I'll find some chokeberry roots and make a gum to stop that bleeding."

He was back in a moment, the roots in his hand. He chewed them silently, until he had reduced the roots to a thick gummy substance, then applied it to the wound. Ripping off a section of her shirt, he fitted the torn strips to her side, knotting them.

His own wound was clotting already, and gave him no trouble.

Then they were moving side by side across a fall of uprooted saplings toward a sluggish stream of water. They entered it together and began to move northwestward. A damp wind whispered through the moss-hung waterways, adding its discomfort to the despair that gripped them. Their clothes were wet. The mud was slippery and treacherous underfoot. A water moccasin might come slithering between the clumps of marsh grass at any time.

"All we need now is to turn a bend in one of these streams and come face to jowls with that damn lobsterback colonel again," Stafford growled.

Colonel Edmund Emerson kicked angrily at the chest that lay on the bottom of the flat-bottomed river boat. It was filled with golden guineas and round silver shillings, but the sight of all that treasure and the knowledge that he had succeeded where other officers had failed aroused no triumph in him. In his own eyes, he had failed. He had been given a chance to put an end to the man who stood between him and Laura Lee, and he had let it slip through his fingers.

Ahead of him, crouched at the prow, he could see Ezra Whipple. The big New Yorker was morose and sullen. Emerson could hear him muttering savagely to himself under his breath.

"Had him in my sights. Three times! Each time I missed."

"The footing was none too good on those logs," Emerson said.

"No matter. I've shot men down before with almost as bad an underfooting. I can't understand the luck that keeps him alive. Just once to have normal conditions when I've got my eyes on him. Just once!"

The Colonel cast a careful glance over his shoulder at the uniformed regular who poled the boat with his heavy, stolid face like a wooden mask. Then he was turning and crouching beside Whipple, whispering softly.

"That chance may be arranged, sooner than you think. How'd you like to have your man at Stafford Hall some fine morning, coming down the steps of the portico, eh?"

Whipple shot his hand out and his thick, hard fingers closed over the Colonel's arm. His eyes were brilliant. "You aren't toying with me, Colonel? That'd be fair cruel, it would."

His excitement was infectious, Emerson decided, feeling his own heart thump in his ribs. "I mean it, Whipple. You and I have waited long enough. It's time to put an end to the farce. I don't know just when or how, but I'll have Billy Joe Stafford at Stafford Hall one of these days."

"Ah," sighed Ezra Whipple, his callused thumb lovingly caressing the hammer of his long rifle. "And when he is, I'll be out in a hazel thicket, putting my sights on him!"

Chapter Eleven

FROM HIS CAMP on Turkey Creek, General Lord Charles Cornwallis took his army southwest in the hope of catching Dan Morgan and his company of sharpshooters before they could join Nathaniel Greene and his rebel militia. If he could find and whip the Virginia and Maryland rifles and set free the five hundred of his own troops that had been captured, it would lessen the sting of Banastre Tarleton's defeat at Cowpens. Cornwallis was no fool. He knew the Americans would run from his superior numbers as a fox from the hounds, and with even greater speed.

Cornwallis ordered his baggage and wagons destroyed.

"We'll march light and fast and live off the land like animals if we must!" he told his officers. "But I want Dan Morgan and I want Nat Greene. Most of all, gentlemen, I want the troops we lost. Attend to it!"

His subordinates attended to it. For once in its life, the British army moved fast. But the Americans were like lightning bolts fleeing before the storm.

General Nathaniel Greene discovered that Cornwallis was throwing everything he had into a headlong chase across the Catawba after Morgan, even as he rode to confer with Dan Morgan at Sherrod's Ford. He sent word by a fast rider: Break camp and come fast! He would join his forces with Morgan's riflemen at Charlotte.

This was late January, 1781, with the sky gray and lowering, the air chill and biting. Cornwallis came north between the Broad and the Catawba, fury cracking the whip that drove his men at a steady stride. Morgan was only a step and a hop ahead of him, aiming for the island ford.

Morgan made the crossing with less than two hours to spare.

Even then, Cornwallis might have snatched back his men who were prisoners of the Americans, but the sun was setting, and rather than risk having his troops wade the rapid currents of the Catawba with American riflemen hidden on the other side, he waited until morning.

113

That night a deluge fell on the land and flooded the river. Cornwallis was forced to wait two days, fuming, until his troops could cross. Morgan took advantage of the delay to ship the prisoners he escorted to Salisbury.

By this time Nat Greene arrived to hurl three hundred North Carolina riflemen under Captain Joseph Graham in a delaying action against the British. Three hundred men could not stop three thousand. Cornwallis crossed the ford, and the chase for the Dan and the resulting ownership of the Carolinas was under way.

Greene sent Dan Morgan flying to the Yadkin. Cornwallis brought his army to Salisbury, to rest for the night. The Americans crossed the trading ford. Hampered by more rain and inundated riverbanks, the English stood helplessly and watched another American army disappear into the February gloom.

Greene and Morgan delayed, feinted, fled. Cornwallis, furious, followed, knowing he must catch and destroy them. Anything less would be fatal, for France was in the war now, and the French fleet was somewhere off the coast. His Tory allies were going into hiding because the rebels were laughing at them, but sometimes they would forget to laugh and then they would burn and kill.

The living chess game went on: a delaying action by a volunteer corps of rebel sharpshooters, the river spilling its swollen waters over its banks and Greene pushing fast toward Guilford Courthouse. Lieutenant Colonel Harry Lee brought his light-horse troops in from Georgetown to join him, with Major Benjamin Huger and Colonel Otho Williams following with their infantry troops, supply wagons, and artillery.

Cornwallis was in an apoplectic fury half the time, raging at nature and the rebels, but retaining enough coolness of mind to ford the Yadkin and stake everything on a desperate gamble. Greene was only twenty-five miles away. The rivers were being swollen by winter rains in the mountains, flooding down into the lowlands. He could catch Greene before Greene reached Virginia to merge his army with that of General Washington, and annihilate him. The weight of superior numbers was on his side. Greene could not flee much longer. There were no more shallow fords, with the rivers in wintertime flood.

The Americans were in a state of exhaustion as they

huddled in damp blankets on the hill slopes somewhat south of Guilford Courthouse. There were men here whose feet oozed red blood, for they had marched mile after mile without shoes or any other protection for their naked feet. Some groaned against the ache of old wounds, brought to life by the damp chill.

The men who followed Morgan—who was himself showing the torture of the rheumatism that plagued him—had come 150 miles from Cowpens. Major Huger had brought his men one hundred miles from their old camp on the Pedee River, over bad clay roads. They lay inert, most of those men, and those who could move about freely cooked what little food they had and brought it to the others.

While the men slept or ate, Nathaniel Greene was arguing with Dan Morgan. "Dan, you can't leave me now! Take command of the light army I've formed. Seven hundred of our best men."

Dan Morgan forced a smile, but his battered face was old and tired, an ashen gray. His uniform was rumpled, its blue cloth stained and discolored. The red clay on his boots and discolored breeches added a note of apathy to the rheumatism and fatigue in him. Abruptly he bent forward, coughing harshly.

When the paroxysm had passed, he shook his head. "It's no use, Nat. I'm done in. I can't think straight any more. All I want is a bed and a good fire. I'm old, Nat. Old!"

Greene strode up and down in the field tent. "Where's Stafford, your next in command? He went through the war with you. If anybody can pull you out of this mood, he can."

"He's gone to find the money Alexander Treat collected for us, Nat. Ah, if we had that! Then the sky wouldn't seem so dark to me."

Greene laughed harshly and went to lift a little velvet purse from the plank desk. He held it out so the candlelight could show its worn threads.

"There's a handful of silver coins in this, Dan. It's what I took from Elizabeth Steele while I was quartered in her house at Salisbury. Two bags of silver coins, she had; the savings of a lifetime. She offered it all to me, to help buy powder and shot, to fight for her liberty as well as our own."

Morgan nodded. "George the Third has all the wealth

of the British Empire behind him. We have only a widow's mite, here and there."

Greene tossed the purse to the desk and brooded at his old friend. "Pray he gets the gold, for God knows we need it." He waited a moment, then said, "And yourself? You won't reconsider?"

Dan Morgan shook his head. "Give the command to Otho Williams, Nat. He's a good man. He fought with Cresap's Virginians. He was in that hellhole prison in New York for a while before we got him back in a prisoner exchange. He knows the South and he'll fight as long as he can sit a horse. Besides, he's eleven years younger than I am."

"Williams? A good choice. I'd name Stafford myself, if he were here, but he isn't. I'll do it, Dan. What about yourself?"

Morgan heaved himself to his feet. He's like an old war-horse, Greene thought, staring at his bulk and his hard face. He smells the battle and he wants to get into it, but he's too tired and his muscles won't do what his mind tells them.

Morgan said heavily, "I'm going to bed. Maybe I'll feel better in the morning."

Morning saw Otho Williams riding out with Harry Lee and his light horse to reconnoiter, while Greene took the rest of his command northward toward the Dan, where it curved upward into Virginia.

It was here, along a stretch of road that wound across hills of red clay, that Billy Joe Stafford and Deborah Treat found them. They had come fast from the Dismal Swamp, once they found their way out of its twisting mosses and interwoven waterways. What was left of the coins in Stafford's shot pouch bought two farm horses. On blanket saddles they had ridden westward, past Halifax and the platform in front of the courthouse where the Declaration of Independence had been read to the farmers and plantation owners in August, 1776. Their way took them through a country of tall oaks and stately sycamores, through rolling red hills and lonely sedge bogs, where the earth was black and rich and alive with pitcher plants and sundews. It was a wild and unconquered land, a rich part of the prize for which men were fighting and dying from Canada to Georgia.

Now they reined in, seeing Harry Lee and his men cantering along the dirt road to Virginia. They let their horses blow, acknowledging the good-natured jeers and comments of the troopers with a wave of their hands.

Debby had managed to find a riding habit of green shag at a border plantation. Her yellow hair was coiled under a tricorn frilled with lace that was slanted down above her left eye. The green jacket that hugged her upper body was open at the throat, to disclose a canary waistcoat and Holland lawn shirt and cravat.

"We'll find Dan Morgan in the rear," Stafford said, reining his big horse around and cantering through the ditches that bordered the road.

His buckskin hunting frock was stained and discolored. The heart was out of Billy Joe Stafford, and he slumped in his saddle with fatigue. More than one night since their debacle in the Dismal Swamp he had walked through the darkness, carrying a sleeping Debby in his arms, seeing the moon come up through the barren branches of a towering oak and listening to the cry of a hunting bobcat or the mournful wail of a distant wolf.

Buying the horses had been a godsend, for he could drowse in the saddle then, against the time when he might need his wits to evade the British or a band of raiding Tories. Two days ago a farmer had told them which way Nat Greene was taking his army; and told them, too, how close Cornwallis was to his heels.

Stafford pulled their horses into a little clearing, letting the troops canter past with a rattle of sabers in scabbards and the rhythmic creak of saddle leather. The smell of trouble hung over everything. These men were tired, close to the breaking point. If he had come back with those chests, their eyes would have been bright and their shoulders straight. He whipped himself, deep inside him, at his failure.

He would have to admit defeat to Dan Morgan and Nat Greene; that, perhaps, was what hurt the most. Dan had been confident that he would bring back the money. Now Dan would get that sick look, the look that had been in his haunted eyes on the plains before Quebec, and again during the awful winter at Valley Forge.

"Master! Master Billy Joe!"

It was a voice out of the past.

Stafford reined around, staring into the dark thickets that bordered the edge of the road. Debby was turning too, crying out, "I heard a voice, Billy Joe! Over there!"

It was Old Gem, his white hair seeming like snow over his round, black head, lunging forward between a clump of flame azaleas and a wild laurel bush. Dismay settled in Stafford. What brought Old Gem this far from the plantation, and in such a mad hurry? Then the slave was grinning and reaching inside his worn woolen jacket, thrusting a letter up into his hands.

Dismay slid away before his curiosity. Stafford turned the letter over and over. The paper was perfumed, and his name was written in Laura Lee's curving, gracious handwriting. In his mind's eye he saw her bent above the mahogany writing desk in the study off the front parlor, nibbling at the quill tip with her small white teeth, frowning a little as she sought to phrase her thoughts.

Impatiently he tore open the envelope.

The words on the paper echoed her voice in his memory, as if she whispered them in his ear. "Billy Joe, dear" . . . in that wheedling manner she had when she wanted something from him very badly. And going on, with a faint pout to her moist red mouth: "I suppose you feel I have been a very naughty girl, being friendly with the British officers who have been making you rich during this silly revolution. Tell me, Billy Joe, how does a wife go about telling her husband he is really the only man she has ever loved, and that whatever she has been stupid and lonely enough to do doesn't really mean a thing?"

His heart thudded softly. "Do you remember the night we spent together by the creek that terribly hot July night, only six years ago? It seems an eternity now, as I remember the way you insisted on soaping me all over and then letting me soap you. Do you remember, Billy Joe darling? I can never forget how sweet and strong and somehow frightening you were that night, in your strength. That memory alone tells me what a foolish wife I have been."

There would be tears in her eyes at this point, he thought. "I cannot and do not ask your forgiveness, but I beg you, I beg you, Billy Joe, for the first time in my life, to understand me. I have been doing a lot of think-

ing lately. I have been wrong, wrong about so many
things. Wrong about you, and wrong about the things you
believe in."

Now her voice would be firm, and there would be
sincerity in it as she rushed on. "Most of all, I failed
to realize that a woman owes her husband the duty of
understanding and following his beliefs rather than her
own. If this sounds as if I have had a change of heart
about being a Tory, and want to become a rebel like yourself, then I am putting down exactly what I feel. I do
want to be a rebel! I do want to believe in this new
young nation you think is being born in this rebellious
war. Not only that, but I am willing to prove my belief
in a tangible way."

Stafford sat rigid in the saddle, reading on, not quite
believing what he saw, but wanting desperately to do
just that. "You remember the chests of gold coins I told
you were buried in the icehouse? Take those chests and
use them as you want. It is your gold, not mine. If it
will buy rifles or shot or food for the men who fight
with you, or warm clothing, or whatever else they may
need to win this war and our independence with it, take
and use it. Can I do any more, Billy Joe?"

"Lord God above!" whispered Stafford, staring blindly
at the paper, feeling exultation flood his cheeks with
blood. "It can't be!"

Eagerly now he read on, seeing Laura Lee smiling trem-
ulously at him, her hands clasped together. "Only come
and reassure me, dearest one, that I am not making a mistake. Tell me that the gold will win us freedom from
the British tyrants. Come and take that gold, gold that
belongs to you. I wish that you would come and take
me, too, but I realize too late that this would be asking
too much of the man I once called husband. Your silly,
stupid Laura Lee."

The breath went out of him and he sagged against
the cantle of his saddle in reaction to the forces that
swept through him. He had failed to get the chests Alexander Treat had buried in the Dismal Swamp, but now
he had two other chests to offer Dan Morgan and Nat
Greene in their place. That gold would change the beaten
look of these tired men who rode to fight the British
until a musket ball ended the ache in their muscles.

He smoothed out the letter, staring down at it.

"It's good news, isn't it, Billy Joe?" asked Debby, her horse sidling closer.

"Good news? Yes, it's good news. I've two chests of golden crowns and sovereigns to offer Greene!"

His explanation of Laura Lee's change of heart brought a frown to her face. Debby shook her head. "It doesn't ring true to me, Billy Joe. Why should she want to be a rebel now?"

His hope made him an ardent advocate. "Because she knows we can win! She will have had word of King's Mountain from me, and news of Cowpens from travelers, or even, perhaps, from her British friends. She'll know we need only money for food and powder and shot to be able to whip the British back into the ocean!"

Debby bit her lower lip. "I still don't think she means it. She has some other reason for writing such news."

"What reason?"

Mistress Treat straightened a little in her pride. She could not tell him that her womanly intuition whispered that Laura Lee Stafford wanted her husband back in her arms; that she had had her fling, and that now she was willing and ready to settle down and become the faithful wife again. Or worse—and at this thought Debby caught her breath—Laura Lee might want to be rid of the encumbrance of a husband who was only a dead weight about her ambitious neck.

"I—I know no reason," she said at last, but her eyes pleaded with him to use his brain, and to examine the motives that would cause a woman like Laura Lee to write him such a letter.

"There is none," Stafford insisted. "She's come to her senses at last, as I always knew she would!"

He grinned and reached out for Debby's hand where it held the rein. "She means nothing to me any more, sweet Deb. She's my wife no longer. But the gold she has hidden in the icehouse—ah, that does mean something. It means better food and warm clothes for all of these men."

Old Gem was nodding at his stirrup. "She tell me herself she want to be rebel woman, Master Billy."

"You see?" Stafford turned to Debby, eyes shining.

Debby nodded, fighting back the panic that told her

Stafford was being desperately blind. Was it the gold or the woman he wanted so desperately to possess? If he put his hands on the gold, would he automatically put his hands on Laura Lee? In his gratitude, a man was often a fool.

Chapter Twelve

STAFFORD CAME DOWN out of the saddle before the pillared portico of Stafford Hall, aware that his heart was banging and thudding just as it had the first time he had ever gone courting a girl. He told himself that he was a fool. He was here to get two chests full of gold coins, and nothing else. It was his memory that played tricks on him, for it kept showing him Laura Lee as he had known her the night they stayed all night at the creek, and the afternoon when he had surprised her wearing only shoes and a new hat before her bedroom mirror.

As his feet touched the driveway gravel, he growled, "I'm as bad as a sailor cooped up on a Baltimore packet on the ocean run. All I seem to be able to think about are the good times I've had here."

There were the bad times, too: the night he had surprised Laura Lee with that British colonel in the bed and the way in which she opened the door to let in soldiers to capture him. He had almost forgotten that, in his haste to put hands on those golden sovereigns. He moved toward the portico and up the wide steps, letting the old hurt and the hate come back into his heart. Laura Lee could play the actress as much as she wanted. All he was after was the gold.

The inner hall was cool and remote, unchanged. Its mahogany butterfly table still gleamed, the carved chairs seemed never to have been moved. Here the outer world stepped lightly, if at all.

Laura Lee was waiting in the front parlor.

Stafford paused in the doorway, staring.

She wore a buckskin hunting frock, almost a pale white, with long fringes at the shoulders and along the sleeves. A green sash, similar to the one that belted his own middle, which was the trade-mark of Morgan's Rifles, circled her waist. Moccasins of Cherokee make and leggings so tight that they seemed painted on her shapely legs completed her costume.

Her soft laughter filled the room as she lifted her arms and twirled for his admiration.

"You like it, Billy Joe? Oh, I knew you would. I knew it!"

The tight buckskin revealed her figure fully. Her heavy breasts bulged outward above a flat stomach, and her round hips printed their shape against the pallid hunting frock. She came toward him, rich red lips smiling faintly, hands reaching for his own.

"I had it made specially for you, Billy Joe. It's some sort of proof that my change of heart is permanent. I copied your uniform and had a tailoress in from the Dan cabins to finish it."

"It becomes you, Laura," he said stiffly. "I only wish you'd had it made a long time ago, if you're sincere about these protestations of yours."

She pouted and smiled, and pulled his arms around her waist, leaning against him. He found her soft and warm, and the touch of her ungirdled flesh made him remember all those things about her that he was trying to forget. Her perfume was heavy with musk, and her rich brown hair was formed into two braids, interwoven with bits of red silk. Unwillingly he admitted he had never seen her look so tempting.

"Don't spoil this for me, Billy Joe." She pouted, eyes laughing up at him. "I've been a bad, silly girl. Help me forget it!"

"What about the gold?"

"You're going to get the gold. Just as soon as you tell me you're glad I've become a rebel."

"Of course I'm glad. I've been trying for five years to make a rebel out of you." He let the bitterness come up into his voice. "You must know how many sleepless nights I've had in the past, from Harlem Heights to King's Mountain, hoping and wishing that you'd see things my way."

Laura Lee put her head against his chest and hugged herself against him. "I'm sorry it took so long. Truly I am."

Stafford stared above her thick brown hair at the Chippendale highboy placed with geometrical precision between the garden windows. Inside him he felt cold, remote. "Let's go get the gold, Laura."

She moved away, turning toward a pedestal table where a silver tray held an engraved glass decanter filled with rich red wine. Beside the tray a matching silver platter was filled with tiny cakes.

"Will you try some wine first, Billy Joe?"

"No wine."

She looked at him and he saw with surprise that tears lay on her long brown lashes. Her smile was tremulous. "Very well, then. The gold."

Brushing past his rigid figure, she went out into the hall. He followed her through the hall, under the spiral staircase, and out the hall door. The herb garden lay brown and barren, with a few stalks of dead plants withered and broken.

The springhouse was a narrow passageway built into a hillside, opening out into a storage room ten feet from the door. Its walls were of heavy stone, and big standing timbers held up its sod roof. It was cool in here. Round wooden tubs of butter were set beside tins of milk, and wooden bins held potatoes and vegetables.

Laura Lee took down a tin candle lamp from a wooden peg in the beam support and held the lamp door open as Stafford struck flint to steel. In a moment the wick was glowing, and she closed and latched the door.

With the lantern held between them, she took him deeper into the slanting tunnel, where a wooden shed formed a protection above the bubbling stream that ran the width of the springhouse. A shovel leaned against the wall.

"Dig where this loose dirt is," she said, kneeling and touching it. "I had Old Gem bury both chests here when they were full."

He took the shovel and thrust it deep into the ground. Within moments, a wood and iron cover lay exposed. Stafford knelt and hefted out the coffer. Turning to the gaping hole, he brought out the second chest. Then Stafford put a hand to the long-barreled pistol in his green sash and turned toward the narrow doorway.

This would be a good time for treachery, he told himself, if there is to be any treachery. It was at a moment like this in the Dismal Swamp that Colonel Edmund Emerson had surprised Debby and himself.

Somewhere in the late-afternoon sunlight, a heron poured its lonely call into the air.

"What are you expecting, Billy Joe? The British?"

Her voice held amusement. Stafford scowled and glanced at her, discovering that she leaned lazily against a cedar upright, her curving hip thrust out mockingly, arms folded across her chest. Her attitude showed no concern, no expectation of armed visitors. Stafford knew her well enough to realize she was not that good an actress.

He grunted and bent for a chest. As he put his hands to the grips on either side, her moccasined foot came down on the coffer top between his hands.

"Why not let Old Gem carry the chests, Billy Joe? Or don't you trust him, either?"

He flushed, kneeling there. "It's just that I can't believe all this, Laura," he told her honestly. "I've been used to considering you a Tory, and to find you giving up gold for the rebel cause—"

She was very close to him, so close that her knee brushed his face as she moved the leg preventing him from lifting the chest.

"You're going to convince me that the 'rebel cause is the right one, Billy Joe," she whispered. "You're going to have dinner with me, and muster all your best arguments. Then, when I am convinced I'm doing the right thing, you'll get your gold."

Stafford came to his feet, frowning.

"Then there is a catch!"

Her eyes opened wide. "Can't you prove to me that the rebels will win this war? Are you so afraid of your own cause that you can't whip up any confidence in its success?"

He was near exasperation. "I've argued and pleaded, threatened and begged you too long to think that now you'd be amenable to reason."

She smiled. "Things have changed lately, Billy Joe, dearest. I'm not the same silly little bride you rode away from five years ago. Or even the same woman you discovered in bed with Colonel Emerson."

"You'll remind me of that?"

She came to stand close to him, head flung back to look up into his face. "Only to prove to you that I have changed! Yes, I was lonely. You know enough about me to understand that. Lonely and frightened. Bewildered. Tories and rebels! Battles being fought because a few hotheads like Sam Adams and Patrick Henry want what they so glibly name liberty! I was confused. I never really gave much thought to the one fact that should have been in my mind all along."

Her body was soft where it leaned against him. Laura Lee had put perfume in the thick brown hair that was braided down over her shoulders .Her smile was as promising and intimate as the slitted eyes that glistened up at him.

"What fact is that?" he asked hoarsely.

"The fact that you're my husband! That I owe you—"

Stafford brought his hands up to her shoulders and pushed her from him. "You'll make me puke, Laura. Do you take me for an idiot, to tell me things like that? I don't deny you've remembered I'm your husband so late in the game, but there's more to the truth than what you tell me."

He bent to lift a heavy coffer and heave it up against his hard middle. He carried it to the front of the icehouse and dropped it. When he turned, Laura Lee was at his elbow.

There was no anger in her, only this strange humility and a sort of hidden fire. Her moccasined toe kicked at the chest.

"Let Old Gem send two slaves to fetch it to the house. You've still to convince me you rebels will win the war!"

He hesitated, and saw mockery in her face. Anger beat through his veins, sluggish and heavy. She played a game with him. Oh, he knew that now. But suddenly the danger of the game did not matter to him. This woman had made a fool and worse of him. His pride was demanding that he let her play out her little drama; play it out until he learned what lurked in her mind. If there was danger to him, he would meet it when it came.

His hand buried itself in her long braids, to hold her head motionless as he brought her in against him, warm and soft.

"Yes," he told her hoarsely, "I still have to convince you. And you have yet to convince me that you're a changed woman, Laura dear!"

Her buckskinned arms slipped about his neck and drew his mouth down close to her lips. "Come up to the house with me, Billy Joe."

The anger in him was growing, but he discovered that

it had become his ally, enabling him to put an arm about her waist and bring her at his side toward the house with convincing eagerness. Her hip moved rhythmically beneath his palm, and for an instant he thought, She thinks she leads me as a mare the stud, helpless to do anything but run after her. She thinks me blind to the fact that nothing but death itself could part her from that yellow gold she's hoarded all during the war.

When would it come, the betrayal that he now felt certain was waiting for him? In the house? Perhaps in the bedroom above the back parlor? A fever mounted in him to hurry that moment of treachery. He understood now why some men became martyrs and embraced the death that awaited them with a smile on their lips.

The house was cool and dark after the warm sunlight. Silence lay over it like a smothering blanket. Faintly they could hear the low singing of the slaves.

As they swung into the parlor, Laura Lee turned and hurled herself against him. Her hot palms framed his cheeks as she whispered hoarsely, "Kiss me now, Billy Joe, the way you used to kiss me when I was your bride! Pretend the years are gone."

It was a way to ensnare his senses, he knew, and make him less alert to the trap he expected to snap shut on him momentarily. In that same blind compulsion that brought him to the house at her side, he bent his mouth to her.

She arched against him, crooning deep in her throat. Against his will, he discovered that his old attraction to her was still alive. It took an effort of will to fight the sweetness flooding his body. If he yielded here, to become the slave to her flesh that he once had been, he would be caught like a fish with the gaff in its scales.

His ears listened for footsteps that would tell him the British were coming for him even as his lips felt the fire of her mouth, but he heard no sound other than the breath that sobbed in her nostrils, and the scratching of her long fingernails on his buckskin hunting frock. God's wounds! What delayed the fools? In a little while, if Laura Lee carried out her game to its promising limits, he would be in no condition to summon Old Gem and the armed slaves who waited in the livery stables at his orders.

Laura Lee drew away and put her flushed cheek to his

face. Her voice whispered close to his ear, "We'll have wine
and cakes, dearest Billy, in the little study."

"Why not upstairs, in the bedroom?" He smiled. "I
think I could convince you ever so much better up there."

Her brown eyes laughed at him. Lazily she pressed
against him. "Upstairs, then, my hungry bridegroom."

Stafford was disappointed. The study would have been
the ideal place to hide British dragoons or foot soldiers,
but the study was empty, except for himself and Laura
Lee. She walked toward the pedestal table that held the
silver tray and glass decanter. It seemed to Stafford that
she was laughing at him silently as she came back across
the carpet carrying the tray and the platter of cookies
before her.

The bedroom was filled with late-afternoon sunlight.
Laura Lee placed the trays on the little night table and
straightened, stretching like a healthy animal. "It's so
warm in here, Billy Joe. Would you mind if I took off
this hunting frock?"

The pale buckskin came up from her hips in her hands,
up her white midriff, and off her shoulders. She tossed
it aside, shaking her head, freeing her hair of the red
ribbons that braided it so that it hung down her back,
seemingly ignorant of the fact that her breasts swung
loosely in the movement.

"There now." She smiled. "I feel a lot easier."

Stafford could not take his eyes from her. He tried to
listen to the silence all around him, waiting for the sound
that would tell him Emerson was coming up the stairs or
down the hall, but this woman was more intoxicating than
the port wine in the glass decanter on the night table.

For an instant he remembered Debby and the sweet
touch of her lips on his mouth, and the love that
gleamed in her blue eyes for him. He cursed the mulish-
ness that had brought him here, knowing he was stepping
into a snare and not caring, if only he could get the gold
that Laura Lee had stored away.

He watched as she bent forward and began to slide
the tight buckskin leggings from her hips. When she
stepped out of them, she moved to the wide bed and
stretched out on it, hands under her head, lost in the
brown hair that spilled over the pillow.

"Sit here beside me, Billy Joe. Tell me all about King's

Mountain and Cowpens, and how the rebels have King George's troops on the run."

The house was still. The singing of the slaves in the open fields, which was a signal Old Gem and he had agreed upon, never faltered. If that singing stopped, it meant the British were riding up the graveled drive to capture him. Lightly he came across the room and seated himself on the edge of the bed.

"If you know about King's Mountain and Cowpens, you know enough," he said hoarsely.

"Gossip has Cornwallis chasing Greene all over the Carolinas, trying to get him to fight."

He smiled wryly. "Let's say that Greene is going north to join his troops with those of General Washington, and that Lord Charley is trying to prevent it."

"Your men are tired and hungry. They need good clothes and shoes and hot food. Maybe powder and shot as well."

His voice was harsh. "You sound like a Tory orator in the streets of Charles Town!"

She brought her gaze down from the underside of the flowered canopy that overhung the bed. "I only repeat rumors. Does the truth about your rebels hurt so much?

"If it does, it's only because of the men who are suffering to win their freedom."

"And freedom is such a precious thing, isn't it, Billy Joe? Freedom from a grasping, stupid king, or freedom from a man whose ideals and ideas have never been your own, or perhaps even freedom from a wife because she is a sore in your flesh, keeping you from loving somebody else."

Stafford stared at her, knowing he was reddening under her taunting gaze. She asked, "Is she so pretty? Lovelier than I? What's she like, this little blonde baggage you've picked up to keep you warm of nights?"

She was laughing at him, taunting him, and the cold thought touched deep into Stafford's brain that she was speaking so freely because it did not matter to her what she said to him. Her words would never return to hurt her through him, because in a little while he would be dead. British soldiers would see to that.

What kept them? Or—and at this conception his flesh crawled in horror—did Laura Lee intend to do the killing herself? Was hers the hand that would put a knife between his ribs as he slept, or her finger the one to trigger a ball between his eyes from a pistol hidden now in a low-boy drawer?

Then her hand came out to cling to his, and she whispered, "I don't blame you in the least, darling. I haven't been a good wife to you since you became a rebel. If you wanted a little camp follower, I'm glad you took her. Even if only to teach me how precious you are to me! That's really what opened my eyes, and made me decide to become a rebel myself, if it would help win you back to me."

His mouth opened in stupefaction. Did she think he would take her back to his bed and board after what she'd done to him?

Laura Lee slid around on the bed to lie with her shoulders in his lap, thick brown hair dangling down to the carpet. Her warm fingers came up across his lips, silencing the words that hung there.

"Don't speak. Not now. Wait a little while, darling. Let me be your bride again, just for this night. Be the way you used to be with me, when there were no such things as armies and battles and men hating each other."

Her whispers ran on in the room, and her soft weight was robbing his brain of its alertness, and the sight of her red mouth and hungry eyes was turning back the years. The sun was dying and its crimson light flooded the room, bringing dimness and a sense of unreality.

Fingertips touched his cheek and slid to his lips. Her voice was in his ears, whispering of what they once had been to each other, drowning out the sound of the singing slaves and the silence of the house, and replacing them with the mad, wild thudding of his heart.

A cry came up from somewhere deep inside him. Then he was turning and bringing her up against him and her mouth was there on his own and there was no mockery in her now but only a crazed, sweet wildness that he dimly remembered out of the years that he thought had been beyond recall.

The dawn light made a paleness in the room as Laura Lee slipped from the blankets where Stafford still slept. The air brought tiny shivers to her flesh as she ran for the buckskin garments she had dropped on the carpet yesterday afternoon. Silently she tugged the leggings on and dropped the hunting frock over her head. As she slipped her feet into the moccasins, she turned toward the bed.

He slept so heavily beside the pillow where her own head had lain! Well, it could be that he was exhausted. She smiled at her remembrances of the night. It had been just as she had wanted. He had played the bridegroom to her bride with all the fevered hunger she could ask, but now that he was to die, she felt no stab of pain or guilt. This had been her leave-taking from Billy Joe Stafford. She had made herself her own parting gift.

Wrapping the green sash about her slim waist, she left the room humming softly. There was need for haste, to bring Edmund and his troops to the house before Billy awakened. She would wait outside, until the volley of shots told her that the Dan River plantation was her own.

Lightly she ran down the spiral stairs and toward the front door.

•

Ezra Whipple shifted restlessly in the laurel thicket that he had made his couch during the night. He had come fast from Turkey Creek on a horse that was hobbled half a mile away in the pine forest. His rifle rested across a fallen log for support.

He felt no tiredness, despite the fact that he had been awake all night. The thirst for vengeance in him was strong enough to chase away sleep.

He ran his palm over the smooth maple stock of the Pennsylvania rifle. It had failed him twice in the past. It would not fail him today. He was leaving nothing to chance. He had propped the barrel on the log so it would not slip or quiver when he pressed the trigger. All he had to do was wait, with the front door of the house three hundred feet ahead of him. When Stafford came out, he would die.

Whipple stiffened and slid down in the rotting underbrush. He put his cheek to the stock and gently took the smooth underside of the barrel in his left hand. His right hand curled about the curving guard as his index finger sought the trigger.

The house door was opening.

Ah! That would be Stafford now, in those pale buckskins with the green sash. Ezra Whipple had seen that Morgan uniform too many times to be mistaken about it at a time like this. He framed the uniform in his sight.

Gently he squeezed the trigger.

Chapter Thirteen

STAFFORD CAME AWAKE to the shot and the scream.
For a moment he lay dazed, head thrust up into the
bright sunlight. There had been a dream, even now trembling on the rim of his consciousness, about Debby and the
swamps and a dark black bird swooping down with the
face of Laura Lee.

He swung out of bed and ran to the window.

The slaves were babbling excitedly by the coach house.
He heard footsteps crunching on the gravel of the drive.
Belatedly he remembered Laura Lee, and turned back to
the empty sheets. The next movement of his eyes revealed the fact that her pale buckskins were missing.

His heart leaped in his chest. That rifle shot from
below!

His hands yanked up his leggings as he ran. The hunting
frock came down over his broad chest as he went down
the staircase three steps at a time. He was knotting the
green sash as his hand thrust the portico door open.

She lay huddled on the steps, her legs bent a little, the
right foot resting on the rim of a tread. Her head hung
down over the third step from the top, and the glory
of her thick brown hair was like a veil covering her face.
Blood dripped from the buckskin jacket to the step.

"Lord God," he whispered, and knelt to lift and cradle
her in his arms.

Her face was waxen and seemed strangely shrunken,
as if the wild, ambitious soul of her had tired at last of its
task. There was pity in him now for her and for the
hungers that made her what she had been. The thing
that she called love had been no more than a gratifica-
tion of the senses, a sensuality of the spirit. Even in the
days of her bridehood, her love for him had been only an
unleashed desire to try her fleshly wisdom with a man.
Laura Lee could never know the clean wild sweetness of
his love for Deborah Treat.

Old Gem was at his elbow, pointing off toward the
woods.

"A man was out there, Master Billy. A big man with
133

black hair. Seen him with the Colonel when he come here before."

"Ezra Whipple!"

Stafford lowered Laura Lee gently to the steps and came to his feet. He whispered, "Take care of her, Gem. I'll be back in a little while." Then he was whirling and moving toward the study behind the parlor.

His long Kentucky rifle was on a wall rack, with his powder horn on its rawhide thong and his hunting knife. He took them down and buckled the knife and belt at his waist. Then, with the rifle in a big hand, he went back the way he had come.

The place where the New Yorker had lain was plain to see, a hollowed spot behind a fallen log. From there his footprints pointed north and west. Stafford began to move at a long stride, following those prints, his eyes held steadily to the forest floor and to the bushes that sprang from its rotting underbrush.

Ezra Whipple had been in no special haste to put Stafford Hall behind him. He did not expect that Billy Joe Stafford was still alive. He had shot at the pale buckskin uniform of Morgan's rifles. He had no way of knowing that Laura Lee Stafford had made herself such a uniform as part of the game she played with her husband. And so he went through the woods at a steady lope, not caring whether his footprints showed.

Stafford tracked as his Cherokee tutor had taught him. He was alive to the broken branch jutting from the trunk of a tree that told him where Whipple had thrust it aside impatiently. His gaze saw and judged the overturned stone as a marker to reveal the fleeing man had slipped. And always his stride was long and sure.

Before the morning sun was well in the sky, he found his man.

Whipple was crouched by a forest spring, face down to the water that gurgled from the earth. He did not hear the soft touch of Stafford's moccasins on the ground, so that when he lifted his face, water still dripping from his gross lips, his eyes bulged wide.

There was horror and superstitious fear mixed with that amazement. Stafford stood in the shadows of a great oak, and his pale buckskins were so white he seemed almost ghostly.

"It ca-can't be! I ki-killed you, back there."

"You killed my wife, you foul vermin."

Blindly Whipple searched with his hand for his rifle, but Stafford was coming at him in a long leap, and his finger-tips only brushed the stock and fell away as he went back-ward. He hit the ground and tried to roll, but Stafford was a leech in his fury.

Legs hooked to the man beneath him, Stafford plunged his hands between the stubble beard and the dirty linen scarf he wore above his homespun jacket. His fingers sank deep into the soft flesh of Whipple's throat and tightened.

Whipple choked and arched his thick body, trying to shake his rider loose.

"You've been wild to get your revenge on me for what I did to you at the Black Thistle," Stafford hissed down at the New Yorker. "You've lusted after Debby—told me what you'd do to her when I died! Well, now's your chance to kill me!"

Whipple's eyes bulged. His chest heaved spasmodically. His hands were locked tight around Stafford's wrists, and the muscles in his arms cracked to the strain he put on them as he sought to pull those hands from his neck.

"Kill me, Whipple! Kill me if you can. Remember, it's the last chance you'll get!"

A frenzy came on Ezra Whipple as the darkness closed in on him. His body contorted savagely, like a spring broken under pressure. His legs lashed out and his big chest exploded upward. Stafford's hands lost their grip and he went backward in rhythm to the wet sob with which Whipple drew air into his agonized lungs.

Whipple came up to a knee and leaped for his rifle where it lay against a jagged rock beside the little forest brook. His hands were closing over it when Stafford fell on him.

There was no endurance left in Ezra Whipple. His lungs still sobbed for the air they had been denied. Under Stafford's shaking his fingers opened and his rifle bounced away. Then he was being turned so that his back was flat on the rock and the hands were there at his throat again and the blackness and the singing in his head were coming back.

"You killed my wife!" Stafford roared at him. "She

wasn't much of a wife, God knows, but you shot her down as if she were a mad dog, without a chance for her life. But you didn't want to kill her, Whipple. You wanted to kill me. What's stopping you now? I'm here, right in front of you!"

Whipple's hands fell away from Stafford's wrists. He tried to talk, but his tongue protruded from his lips like a thick gag.

"Kill me, damn you! Kill me, as you've tried to do before. Or isn't it your style to kill a man when you're face to face with him, unless he's smaller than you or unarmed? Every time you've tried to kill me it's been from cover!"

Ezra Whipple bent back and back. Now his hair was touching the cold forest water in the brook. Then his forehead. When his mouth went under, he was dead.

Stafford clung to him for uncounted minutes, whispering down at him between his teeth. Then he opened his hands and the body slid sideways a little, limp and loose.

He knelt back and lifted his head and felt the cold March wind on his face. Dazedly he stared around him, seeing the blue sky overhead and the barren tree branches above him. Then he looked down at the dead man and felt sick.

A madness had been in him while he fought. His thoughts had been a jumble of visions: Debby trying to claw herself free of this man at the Black Thistle ordinary, and Whipple hissing his hate as they fought in the tavern at Winnsboro, and a remembrance of the Dismal Swamp when Whipple had scratched a rifle ball on his arm and another ball across Debby's flesh, making it bleed. The pain etched on Debby's face while he had bandaged her was always before him, together with the fright in her eyes when she thought of this man. At last he realized that he had killed Ezra Whipple in such a frenzy, not because of what he had done to Laura Lee, but because of what he had threatened to do to Debby.

He stood up and breathed deeply of the fragrant forest air. Whipple would have died with a rifle bullet in him if he had just been avenging Laura Lee's death. He would have stood off and shot him down without compassion. It had been Debby in his blood that had driven him to madness.

He was free now to marry her. Laura Lee was gone and the Dan plantation was all his own, with no other voice or hand to question his authority. He would find Debby and marry her and bring her back to live while he finished out the war with Morgan's Rifles.

Exultation blossomed in him. He began to run with the loose, loping stride of an Indian through the forest.

The March wind was biting hard through torn homespun and stinging fingers and faces as the Continentals trudged along the dirt roads leading south from Virginia into the Carolinas. These were the riflemen and the colonial militia who had come north along these same roads less than a month before, during Nathaniel Greene's two-hundred-mile retreat from Charlotte, a feat accomplished with Cornwallis engaging his rear guard almost daily, with temperatures near the zero mark, and with men starved for food and rest.

Now these same men were coming back to fight again.

Lee and Pickens were already at work near the Haw, their light cavalry making bloody excursions at Cornwallis' wings. They caught Colonel Pyle and smashed his Tory forces close by the old Salisbury road, with Pyle himself hiding in a pond with only his nose above water to escape capture. Tarleton and his Green Horse troops had been driven back to Hillsboro. The stage was being set for Greene and his riflemen to engage the British in the battle that rebel headquarters was hoping would break the English back in the South.

Friends were coming into that thin rebel line hourly, bringing word that Cornwallis was desperately foraging for food. His men were going from house to house in Hillsboro, robbing inhabitants of their stores. He was flinging Banastre Tarleton out in sallies, seeking to stem the oncoming army. Caught by the light-horse dragoons under Harry Lee and a company of picked riflemen under Preston, Tarleton lost thirty men without wounding a single American. With masterful skill, General Greene disposed his forces in flanking movements from Guilford all the way to Troublesome Creek, until Cornwallis thought that his army was three times larger than it actually was.

Cornwallis wanted to fight, despite what he thought were frightening odds, for by this time the frustration of chasing Greene and never quite catching him was gnawing inside him. He brought his regulars up from the New Garden meetinghouse northward toward Guilford Courthouse. The land sloped here in gently rolling meadows from the great Salisbury road to the courthouse itself. An oak forest stretched away on either side of the road.

The Americans waited for the lobsterbacks behind fence rails and trees just at the edge of this wood. Four regiments of the Virginia Continentals waited at the courthouse, with the wide meadows ahead of them. They could see the British veterans marching as at parade, four abreast as they came striding with the sunlight glinting on bayonets and buttons.

The artillery began it, but the rifles of the North Carolinians picked up the barrage from behind their fence rails. Cornwallis hurled a bayonet attack at these hidden troops, and the struggle began to spread across the fields to Lee's light horse and Campbell's riflemen.

Many of the American troops were inexperienced farm boys, newly recruited. The sight of naked bayonets flashing at them drove cold fear down their backs. They threw away knapsacks and canteens and fled.

The veteran Virginians and Marylanders held firm. Their long rifles raked the long red lines of attacking British infantry with a terrible hail of lead. Men went face down in the fields and lay unmoving. Colonel Washington and his light horse came sweeping through the March morning with sabers flashing, just as the Delaware brigade under Captain Kirkwood felt the full fury of the British charge.

The field was a mass of gray smoke and moving red uniforms, of silent men in pale buckskin kneeling to pour their rifle fire into the lines of charging English regulars.

Billy Joe Stafford fought with recently appointed Brigadier General Otho Williams' Virginians. He knelt to fire and reload, tapping his powder horn against the muzzle of his Kentucky rifle and ramming home the patch with a practiced wrist. He saw a bayonet charge break less than twenty feet away when the red flame from the Virginia and Maryland rifles decimated its ranks, and watched men whirl and run for the safety of the distant woods.

As the first British lines broke, the second and third moved up, rifles held in steady hands, bayonets low for stabbing. An officer went down with red blood spouting from his throat. Men dropped and lay unmoving where they fell.

It was then, just as he fired and saw his man reel from his ball, that Colonel Emerson appeared. He was on foot, saber waving overhead, his face turning to shout encouragement at his troops. Stafford stared unbelieving, aware that a thick, hot delight was gripping his lungs, holding him motionless, his smoking rifle still unloaded.

"God's love," he breathed, and let his rifle slide from his fingers.

His right hand went down and closed on the bone haft of his long hunting knife, dragging it from its deerskin sheath. Then he was crawling forward on toes and hands, moving out from behind the stone fence where the Virginians lay, sliding through the low-hanging gun smoke, keeping his gaze always on the British colonel.

That man with the polished black boots and taut breeches, the silver buttons and red uniform jacket, his mouth open in a shout, was the man who had stationed Ezra Whipple outside the mansion to kill him. Whipple's finger had squeezed the trigger, but the Colonel was as much the murderer of Laura Lee as the New Yorker. Stafford felt a wild cry rise in his throat as he hurled himself forward.

Emerson turned, his saber cutting sideways.

The saber grated on the blade of his hunting knife. Then Stafford was in close and stabbing, and Emerson grunted and tore away.

They went down, rolling past the gaitered legs of the British regulars. They brought up hard against the piled stones that formed the bulwark over which the Virginia rifles were spitting their red flames. Emerson dropped his saber and clutched blindly for Stafford's knife hand. Locked hand to hand they clung and panted, straining.

"Damn your eyes, Emerson," whispered Stafford. "Your man Whipple killed Laura Lee before I broke his neck!"

"Laura!"

It was a shocked sound, a gasped protest against that awesome trick of fate. Stafford laughed between clenched teeth. "Spoils everything you'd planned, doesn't it? Laura's dead and can do you no good now. The plantation will never be yours even if you kill me here!"

Emerson sobbed oaths and writhed furiously, straining. There was madness in Stafford's eyes as they glinted down at him.

Bullets whistled overhead. Once a Virginian's rifle fired so close to Stafford's ears that he was deafened. A British bayonet came stabbing down, just missing his buckskinned leg. Men cursed and fought and died as those two rolled among them, jarring against the rock ledge of the Americans, slamming into the buckling legs of a dying British regular. Powder smoke was all around them, thick and gray.

Emerson was weakening. His body was not the thing of bone and whipcord muscle that Stafford's body was. That glittering blade above him was coming always closer. Now the point was at his chest. Now it was cutting into the cloth of his white waistcoat so that he felt the kiss of the steel.

"God! Stafford, wait! Not here, not like this! I don't want to die!"

"Neither did Laura Lee!"

"I didn't mean to kill her."

"It was me the New Yorker aimed at! Laura'd made a twin of the buckskin uniform I wear. He thought she was I."

Emerson's straining arms gave way. A foot of bright steel came down hard into his chest. His body twitched, thrusting upward, but he could not dislodge the man who clung to him like a physician's leech. And then he went limp and his head fell sideways.

Stafford slowly came out of the mad frenzy that had held him prisoner as he fought with Emerson. His eyes took in the advancing English troops, the rigid bayonets, the hard faces under the towering black peaks. A Virginian was shouting hysterically at him from behind the rocks.

He left his knife where it was and went scrambling back and up and over the stones. Two musket balls hit the rocks and ricocheted sideways just as he perched on the top, before he fell over.

A rifle captain bent and hissed, "We're moving back! Got orders to cover the retreat."

Stafford's fumbling hand found his rifle. Then he was assessing the situation with hard cold eyes and snapping the orders that would bring this thin line of Virginia veterans out from behind their stone fences to cover the withdrawal.

American ammunition was running low after two hours of hard fighting. Stafford found himself remembering his failure in the Dismal Swamp. If he had been able to get the money Alexander Treat had collected back in '74, there would have been enough shot and ball in the pouches and enough powder in the powder horns to finish off Cornwallis forever this afternoon. The money he brought from the Stafford plantation was on its way north now to buy that needed ammunition. But the shot and French powder would never get here in time for that.

His Virginians fell back, firing steadily as their lines folded in on each other. The artillery was being abandoned for lack of horses to drag the cannon. Stafford knew what was in Nat Greene's mind without being told: He was afraid to risk the loss of this army, as Horatio Gates had lost an army at Camden. Soldiers without ammunition are not soldiers at all. It would serve American liberty better to run today and fight another time, when these ragged men had something in their hands with which to fight.

And so Nathaniel Greene retreated while the Virginia rifles covered his rear.

Cornwallis was afraid to pursue. He had lost more than six hundred men, not counting the officers who had dropped to that deadly rifle fire. The Americans had lost less than half that number, and a large part of their casualties were wounded, rather than dead men. If the Americans had not retreated, it would have been a rousing victory for them. But retreat they did, and so Lord Charles Cornwallis claimed the victory.

It was a disastrous victory. In Parliament, British statesmen declaimed that one more such triumph would leave Britain without an army, and began to talk of peace between the mother country and its colonies.

Lord Cornwallis was no fool. He knew that Guilford Courthouse had cost him the South. Now he must march north for reinforcements, and to make contact with the British fleet. The Loyalists in the South were in hiding. Nothing could be gained by staying below the Dan River much longer.

Within six months, he would be at Yorktown.

Chapter Fourteen

THE BEDROOM was silent at this hour of early dusk, except for the sobs of the girl who lay stretched across the counterpane of the canopy bed. She knew a fierce anger at her own squeamishness, which had made her flee like a startled doe when Billy Joe Stafford rode off to meet his wife. Her little fist slammed down again and again at the soft mattress that held her shaking body.

"I should have been brave enough to wait for him," she whispered against the tear-stained pillow. "Brave or —shameless! I want him so much! And yet I let him walk off to that hussy without even putting up a fight to keep him!"

The thought of her self-sacrifice brought a new flood of tears that she attempted to stifle in the pillow, rolling her blonde head from side to side. If only she weren't so proud! If only she could really be like the little camp follower she had pretended to be when she first met Billy Joe! *That* one would have waited for him to come back. If he had not come back, she would have gone after him.

"Now I've lost him forever," she wailed, and rolled over on her back.

A bellow from belowstairs brought her up to a sitting position on the bed. The roar came again, echoed by the shouts of several men. Feet pounded on the inn stairs and then a fist was hammering at her door.

A voice roared in the hall and the fist came banging against the planks with enough force to shake the walls.

"Open up inside, Deborah Treat, before I kick this door down!"

Dear Lord in Heaven! Debby came off the bed in her bare feet and trembled. She wore only a thin silken shift, and that was Billy Joe Stafford himself out there, demanding admittance. Her heart thumped crazily. Her hands shook. Tears of joy and happiness ran down her cheeks.

"Deborah Treat! I'm waiting!" came the roar again.

"Y-yes, Billy Joe. I h-hear you!"

142

"Then open the door before I kick it open."

"But I'm not d-dressed! Not p-properly, that is."

"All the better!"

She ran to the door and slipped the latch and stood back as the door opened and closed. Billy Joe was there, towering in his pale buckskins, and his blue eyes were hot as they ran down her body, which the thin silk did nothing to hide. He grinned and his arms went out and then she was being crushed against him and his lips were like a fire on her own, roving to her soft throat and then to the cool upper swells of her bosom.

"Please, Billy Joe. Please let me down. This is disgraceful!"

"Disgraceful and wonderful and I'm happier than I've ever been before in my life! I ought to be sad, because Laura Lee is dead, along with Ezra Whipple and Colonel Emerson—but I'm not!"

She tried to plead with him, to put into words the questions that came storming into her head, but how can a woman speak with a man's lips holding her mouth? And with a man's arms crushing the air from her lungs, holding her so tight against him?

"Bi—"

"I came direct from Guilford Courthouse."

"Plea—"

"I didn't stop for anything. I wore out a horse chasing you to this inn!"

She gave up and lay against him, letting him hold her crushed to his chest, smiling as his lips whispered against her throat, "Now you're coming back with me to the Dan. You're going to be mistress of Stafford Hall, and raise little Staffords with me."

Her laughter was throaty as she breathed, "You haven't even proposed yet!"

"There's a church down the street, and a preacher to be found in the morning."

"In the morning? But what about tonight?"

He eyed her with sly blue eyes. "The inn's full up. I've no place to sleep save your big bed yonder. It seems to me that a future husband merits some consideration. Of course, I could sleep on the cold bare ground outside."

"No." She laughed softly. "You won't have to sleep on the cold bare ground."

As he lifted and carried her toward the canopy bed, Debby thought that neither of them was going to do any sleeping this night.

THE END